WITHDRAWN

CHARLES
CHESNUTT

CHARLES CHESNUTT

Cliff Thompson

Senior Consulting Editor
Nathan Irvin Huggins
Director
W.E.B. Du Bois Institute for Afro-American Research
Harvard University

CHELSEA HOUSE PUBLISHERS
New York   Philadelphia

Chelsea House Publishers
Editor-in-Chief Remmel Nunn
Managing Editor Karyn Gullen Browne
Picture Editor Adrian G. Allen
Art Director Maria Epes
Assistant Art Director Howard Brotman
Manufacturing Director Gerald Levine
Systems Manager Lindsey Ottman
Production Manager Joseph Romano
Production Coordinator Marie Claire Cebrián

Black Americans of Achievement
Senior Editor Richard Rennert

Staff for CHARLES CHESNUTT
Text Editor Marian W. Taylor
Copy Editor Ian Wilker
Editorial Assistant Michele Berezansky
Designer Diana Blume
Picture Researcher Pat Burns
Cover Illustration Daniel Mark Duffy

First Printing

1 3 5 7 9 8 6 4 2

Library of Congress Cataloging-in-Publication Data
Thompson, Cliff.
   Charles Waddell Chesnutt, author/by Cliff Thompson
   p.   cm.—(Black Americans of achievement)
   Includes bibliographical references and index.
   Summary: Discusses the life and writings of the early
twentieth-century black author whose novels examine
the Afro-American experience.
ISBN 1-55546-578-1.
        0-7910-0235-7 (pbk.)
   1. Chesnutt, Charles Waddell, 1858–1932—Juvenile literature.
2. Novelists, American—19th century—Biography—Juvenile
literature. 3. Afro-Americans in literature—Juvenile literature.
[1. Chesnutt, Charles Waddell, 1858–1932. 2. Authors, American.
3. Afro-Americans—Biography.] I. Title. II. Series.
PS1292.C6Z89   199291-33273
813'.4—dc20   CIP
[B]   AC

Frontispiece:
*Charles Chesnutt—novelist,
short-story writer, essayist, and
tireless crusader for universal human
rights—works on a manuscript in
the study of his Cleveland, Ohio,
home in 1910.*

CONTENTS

BLACK AMERICANS OF ACHIEVEMENT

HANK AARON
baseball great

KAREEM ABDUL-JABBAR
basketball great

RALPH ABERNATHY
civil rights leader

ALVIN AILEY
choreographer

MUHAMMAD ALI
heavyweight champion

RICHARD ALLEN
religious leader and social activist

MAYA ANGELOU
author

LOUIS ARMSTRONG
musician

ARTHUR ASHE
tennis great

JOSEPHINE BAKER
entertainer

JAMES BALDWIN
author

BENJAMIN BANNEKER
scientist and mathematician

AMIRI BARAKA
poet and playwright

COUNT BASIE
bandleader and composer

ROMARE BEARDEN
artist

JAMES BECKWOURTH
frontiersman

MARY MCLEOD BETHUNE
educator

JULIAN BOND
civil rights leader and politician

GWENDOLYN BROOKS
poet

JIM BROWN
football great

BLANCHE BRUCE
politician

RALPH BUNCHE
diplomat

STOKELY CARMICHAEL
civil rights leader

GEORGE WASHINGTON CARVER
botanist

RAY CHARLES
musician

CHARLES CHESNUTT
author

JOHN COLTRANE
musician

BILL COSBY
entertainer

PAUL CUFFE
merchant and abolitionist

COUNTEE CULLEN
poet

ANGELA DAVIS
civil rights leader

BENJAMIN DAVIS, SR., AND BENJAMIN DAVIS, JR.
military leaders

SAMMY DAVIS, JR.
entertainer

FATHER DIVINE
religious leader

FREDERICK DOUGLASS
abolitionist editor

CHARLES DREW
physician

W.E.B. DU BOIS
scholar and activist

PAUL LAURENCE DUNBAR
poet

KATHERINE DUNHAM
dancer and choreographer

DUKE ELLINGTON
bandleader and composer

RALPH ELLISON
author

JULIUS ERVING
basketball great

JAMES FARMER
civil rights leader

ELLA FITZGERALD
singer

MARCUS GARVEY
black nationalist leader

JOSH GIBSON
baseball great

DIZZY GILLESPIE
musician

PRINCE HALL
social reformer

W. C. HANDY
father of the blues

WILLIAM HASTIE
educator and politician

MATTHEW HENSON
explorer

CHESTER HIMES
author

BILLIE HOLIDAY
singer

JOHN HOPE
educator

LENA HORNE
entertainer

LANGSTON HUGHES
poet

ZORA NEALE HURSTON
author

JESSE JACKSON
civil rights leader and politician

MICHAEL JACKSON
entertainer

JACK JOHNSON
heavyweight champion

JAMES WELDON JOHNSON
author

SCOTT JOPLIN
composer

BARBARA JORDAN
politician

CORETTA SCOTT KING
civil rights leader

MARTIN LUTHER KING, JR.
civil rights leader

SPIKE LEE
filmmaker

REGINALD LEWIS
entrepreneur

ALAIN LOCKE
scholar and educator

JOE LOUIS
heavyweight champion

RONALD MCNAIR
astronaut

MALCOLM X
militant black leader

THURGOOD MARSHALL
Supreme Court justice

TONI MORRISON
author

CONSTANCE BAKER
MOTLEY
*civil rights leader
and judge*

ELIJAH MUHAMMAD
religious leader

EDDIE MURPHY
entertainer

JESSE OWENS
champion athlete

SATCHEL PAIGE
baseball great

CHARLIE PARKER
musician

GORDON PARKS
photographer

ROSA PARKS
civil rights leader

SIDNEY POITIER
actor

ADAM CLAYTON
POWELL, JR.
political leader

COLIN POWELL
military leader

LEONTYNE PRICE
opera singer

A. PHILIP RANDOLPH
labor leader

PAUL ROBESON
singer and actor

JACKIE ROBINSON
baseball great

DIANA ROSS
entertainer

BILL RUSSELL
basketball great

JOHN RUSSWURM
publisher

SOJOURNER TRUTH
antislavery activist

HARRIET TUBMAN
antislavery activist

NAT TURNER
slave revolt leader

DENMARK VESEY
slave revolt leader

ALICE WALKER
author

MADAM C. J. WALKER
entrepreneur

BOOKER T. WASHINGTON
educator and racial spokesman

IDA WELLS-BARNETT
civil rights leader

WALTER WHITE
civil rights leader

OPRAH WINFREY
entertainer

STEVIE WONDER
musician

RICHARD WRIGHT
author

ON
ACHIEVEMENT
———— ❧ ————

Coretta Scott King

BEFORE YOU BEGIN this book, I hope you will ask yourself what the word *excellence* means to you. I think that it's a question we should all ask, and keep asking as we grow older and change. Because the truest answer to it should never change. When you think of excellence, perhaps you think of success at work; or of becoming wealthy; or meeting the right person, getting married, and having a good family life.

Those important goals are worth striving for, but there is a better way to look at excellence. As Martin Luther King, Jr., said in one of his last sermons, "I want you to be first in love. I want you to be first in moral excellence. I want you to be first in generosity. If you want to be important, wonderful. If you want to be great, wonderful. But recognize that he who is greatest among you shall be your servant."

My husband, Martin Luther King, Jr., knew that the true meaning of achievement is service. When I met him, in 1952, he was already ordained as a Baptist preacher and was working toward a doctoral degree at Boston University. I was studying at the New England Conservatory and dreamed of accomplishments in music. We married a year later, and after I graduated the following year we moved to Montgomery, Alabama. We didn't know it then, but our notions of achievement were about to undergo a dramatic change.

You may have read or heard about what happened next. What began with the boycott of a local bus line grew into a national movement, and by the time he was assassinated in 1968 my husband had fashioned a black movement powerful enough to shatter forever the practice of racial segregation. What you may not have read about is where he got his method for resisting injustice without compromising his religious beliefs.

He adopted the strategy of nonviolence from a man of a different race, who lived in a different country, and even practiced a different religion. The man was Mahatma Gandhi, the great leader of India, who devoted his life to serving humanity in the spirit of love and nonviolence. It was in these principles that Martin discovered his method for social reform. More than anything else, those two principles were the key to his achievements.

This book is about black Americans who served society through the excellence of their achievements. It forms a part of the rich history of black men and women in America—a history of stunning accomplishments in every field of human endeavor, from literature and art to science, industry, education, diplomacy, athletics, jurisprudence, even polar exploration.

Not all of the people in this history had the same ideals, but I think you will find something that all of them had in common. Like Martin Luther King, Jr., they all decided to become "drum majors" and serve humanity. In that principle—whether it was expressed in books, inventions, or song—they found something outside themselves to use as a goal and a guide. Something that showed them a way to serve others, instead of only living for themselves.

Reading the stories of these courageous men and women not only helps us discover the principles that we will use to guide our own lives but also teaches us about our black heritage and about America itself. It is crucial for us to know the heroes and heroines of our history and to realize that the price we paid in our struggle for equality in America was dear. But we must also understand that we have gotten as far as we have partly because America's democratic system and ideals made it possible.

We are still struggling with racism and prejudice. But the great men and women in this series are a tribute to the spirit of our democratic ideals and the system in which they have flourished. And that makes their stories special and worth knowing. ❧

1

THE GAMBLE

I N THE SPRING of 1883, 24-year-old Charles Chesnutt took the biggest risk of his life. He boarded a northbound train in Fayetteville, North Carolina, leaving behind his family and friends, as well as his prestigious job as a school principal, for the chance to work in New York City. As soon as he settled in, he would send for his wife, Susan, who was pregnant with their third child, and his daughters, Ethel and Helen. But would he be able to find a job in New York? Most of his acquaintances in Fayetteville had advised him not to go; a young black southerner, they said, would have little hope of success in such a place.

As his train roared north, Chesnutt must have wondered if his neighbors were right. But right or wrong, he had to go through with his plan. There was nothing more for him in Fayetteville: He had learned all that its schools would teach him, and his teaching career had already reached its peak. Furthermore, he wanted to raise his children in a society where their skills and qualities were valued, not among people who considered their black blood a "taint."

Chesnutt was not expecting miracles from the North, but he knew that blacks there had at least a chance of improving their lot. In the segregated South, no such chance existed. There, for example, he could teach only in an impoverished "colored

At the age of 24, Charles Chesnutt was a husband and father, a homeowner, and the well-paid principal of a North Carolina teachers college—but he wanted more. In 1883 he headed for New York City and, he hoped, a career as a writer.

school," although he had proved himself an exceptionally able teacher. The highest professional recommendation he had ever received was: "His morality is high toned, and although colored, he is a gentleman."

Chesnutt would never forget an overheard conversation between one of his friends and a local white storekeeper, who had asked the friend "what kind of a fellow" Chesnutt was.

"Well sir," the friend had responded, "he's a perfect gentleman in every respect; I don't know his superior."

"Why, he's a nigger, ain't he?" the storekeeper had said. "Does he think he's as good as a white man?"

"Every bit of it, sir," the friend had answered.

"Well, he's a nigger," said the white man, "and with me a nigger is a nigger, and nothing in the world can make him anything else but a nigger."

Chesnutt harbored ambitions of becoming a writer; one of his earliest literary efforts was a humorous but bitter poem on this subject. Entitled "A Perplexed Nigger," it ends with the verse:

Perhaps some wise man of the white folks,
Will make the mystery plain,
Why justice and Christian charity,
Are different for different men;
Why they set us aside in the churches
And even in the common schools,
And in the insane asylums,
They separate even the fools!

The young teacher planned to make his mark on the world and, he wrote in his journal, to "serve my race better in some more congenial occupation." After taking inventory of his talents, he had decided his best bet was literature: He liked to write; he had something to say and, he believed, the ability to say it well; he could write without investing in further training; and, finally, he thought writing could make him rich. Having decided what to do, he had thought about where to do it: New York City seemed the obvious place for a writer's headquarters. Could he succeed in the nation's biggest, busiest metropolis?

At first, it seemed that he could. He stepped off the train and right into a job, signing on almost immediately as a reporter for Dow, Jones and Company, then a Wall Street news agency. He also worked for a daily newspaper, the *New York Mail and Express*, interviewing New York's top financial men.

Recalling these days, Chesnutt later wrote with amusement, "I often wonder, when I read newspaper comments on stock market conditions and prospects, whether any of them were written by green young men from the country, with as little knowledge of

Pedestrians, trolley cars, and horse-drawn trucks jockey for space near Manhattan's Wall Street in the 1880s. Chesnutt landed a good job as a New York financial reporter, but he considered the crowded city a bad place to raise a family and left after eight months.

finance as I had." But green or not, Chesnutt was getting paid to write, living from paycheck to paycheck in his rented room in New York City.

Six months after his arrival, a letter from Susan Chesnutt announced the birth of Edwin, the couple's third child. Charles Chesnutt now felt more pressure than ever to make things better for his family. His salary was enough to feed himself and send money home, but he was not making enough to support five people in New York. Besides, for all its glamour and promise, this city of 4 million people was dangerous and unpredictable, not the place where Chesnutt wanted to raise his children.

The young husband and father missed his family fiercely; just as fiercely, however, he refused to accept defeat and return to the South. He would find a good job somewhere in the North, then reassemble his little flock. As Christmas 1883 approached, he resigned from his 2 jobs, packed his bag, boarded another train, and headed for the city where he had been born 25 years earlier.

Chesnutt arrived in Cleveland, Ohio, in an icy rainstorm, and took a long look at the city where he would live the rest of his days. Bristling with smokestacks, Cleveland was a rapidly growing center of industry, boasting a profusion of steel mills, lumberyards, railroads, and oil refineries. Chesnutt soon landed a job in the accounting department of the Nickel Plate Railroad Company, where he took dictation, typed letters, and totaled accounts. The work paid well, and he saved almost every penny, trying to speed the day when he could send for his wife and children.

Susan Chesnutt, who also ached for the reunion, wrote her husband a touching letter in early 1884. "How I long to be with you once more," she said. "I have found out since you left what you were to me. You were a companion, and you knew me better even

A Nickel Plate Railroad supervisor awaits a train in Cleveland, Ohio, around 1885. Working for the Nickel Plate as a secretary-accountant, Chesnutt soon saved enough money to rent and furnish a small house, send for his wife and children, and start a new life in the city where he had been born in 1858.

than my father or mother, or at least you were more in sympathy with me than anybody else, and my failings were overlooked. No one can tell, my dearest husband, how I miss that companionship. God grant that we may not be separated much longer, for I cannot stand it, I am afraid."

In April 1884, Chesnutt rented a small house for $16 per month, filled it with secondhand furniture, bought new curtains, and laid in a stock of food, coal for heat, and coal oil for the lamps. In the middle of the month, he traveled to Richmond, Virginia, met Susan and the children, and escorted them to their new home.

The family settled into life in Cleveland, where they formed part of the city's tiny black population. Although midwestern whites discriminated against blacks in some areas—certain residential sections of Cleveland, for example, were clearly off-limits to blacks—the Chesnutts found their neighbors, who were of mixed races, to be friendly and welcoming. Charles Chesnutt felt certain he had come to a place where he could bring up his children in peace, a city where he could develop his talents and realize his dreams. The next few years would test that certainty. ✺

2

"I WILL LIVE DOWN THE PREJUDICE"

CHARLES WADDELL CHESNUTT was born in Cleveland, Ohio, on June 20, 1858, the first of Anne Maria and Andrew Jackson Chesnutt's three sons and two daughters. Natives of Fayetteville, North Carolina, Anne Maria and Andrew were both freeborn *mulattoes*, people of mixed racial ancestry.

Andrew Chesnutt's father, tobacco farmer Waddell Cade, was a wealthy white slaveholder with two distinct families. Along with the children he had sired by his late wife, Cade supported the children—who included Andrew—born to him and his housekeeper, a free black woman named Ann Chesnutt.

Under the social and legal codes of the pre–Civil War South, white men could, and often did, keep black mistresses, but interracial marriage was not only socially unacceptable but illegal. Thus, although Cade was a widower and apparently devoted to Chesnutt, he could never make her his wife.

A fraction of the area's blacks and mulattoes had gained their freedom, but none could hope to vote or achieve economic or social equality. By the time Andrew Chesnutt reached young manhood, he wanted more from life than this; in 1856, he and a small group of like-minded, free people of color decided to seek their fortune in the West.

Included in the traveling party were a young woman named Anne Maria Sampson and her mother, Chloe. As they approached Ohio, Anne

Seven-year-old Charles Chesnutt (left) protectively holds the hand of his younger brother, Lewis, in 1865. Later that year, the Chesnutt family moved from Cleveland, Ohio, where this photograph was taken, to Fayetteville, North Carolina, where the boys grew up.

Andrew Jackson Chesnutt—like his wife, the product of mixed racial ancestry—named his son, Charles Waddell Chesnutt, after his own father, slave-owning North Carolina farmer Waddell Cade.

Maria and Andrew fell in love; when they reached Cleveland, they married. Andrew found work running a horse-drawn bus and settled down with his bride and her mother, who had bought a house on Cleveland's Hudson Street. Charles arrived a year later. A few months after that, the Chesnutts moved to the nearby town of Oberlin, site of Oberlin College.

Predominantly white, Oberlin's population included a large number of *abolitionists*, or opponents of slavery. Oberlin College had been the first American educational institution to admit black students, and the town itself was a "station" on the Underground Railroad, the informal network of safe houses where escaped slaves could count on concealment and aid.

On September 13, 1858, a few weeks after the Chesnutts' arrival in Oberlin, two bounty hunters and a United States marshal rode into the neighborhood in search of a fugitive slave. They captured him near the edge of town. The act enraged Oberliners, some of whom formed a posse and rode to the rescue. Catching up with the slave and his captors in nearby Wellington, the men of Oberlin bound the hunters hand and foot, then set the slave free. Among his deliverers were a professor, several students, and Andrew Jackson Chesnutt.

Chesnutt and his family had adapted easily to the Ohio town and its liberty-loving people. Earning a living there, however, proved harder. After the family's second son, Lewis, arrived in late 1860, Andrew moved his wife and children back to his mother-in-law's house in Cleveland. He regained his old job, but this time he would keep it for only a few months.

In April 1861, the federal garrison at South Carolina's Fort Sumter fell to insurgent southern troops, and America went to war with itself. Heeding President Abraham Lincoln's urgent call for militiamen, tens of thousands of northerners enlisted in their state regiments, which at that point accepted only white volunteers. Although slavery—often termed the "peculiar institution"—was the focal point of the Civil War, neither the North nor the South trusted blacks enough to arm them.

Yet the nation's black population, speaking through such articulate leaders as former slave Frederick Douglass, insisted on participating in the war. "Let the blacks and free colored people be called into service and formed into a liberating army!" Douglass demanded.

Serving as scouts, intelligence agents, nurses, and guerrillas, black men and women took part in the northern war effort from the beginning. Not until Congress passed the Militia Act of July 1862, however, did the government make black troop enlistment official. "Ironically," points out historian James C. Mohr, "Afro-Americans had to struggle for the right to die in the one war that affected them more dramatically than any other in American history."

Even after Congress legalized their military status, blacks continued to suffer from racist attitudes, which were often as harsh in the North as they were in the South. Black soldiers were segregated, paid less than whites, commanded only by white officers, and employed largely as laborers. As the war went on, black units (notably the celebrated 54th Massachusetts) proved their courage and military skill time and again, but acceptance by their white counterparts still came slowly and grudgingly.

Too young to understand these things at the time, Charles Chesnutt would absorb them as he grew up. He heard tales of the war, of black heroes, of injustice, of friendship between the races; he would listen, remember, and, ultimately, make use of them. The nation's racial attitudes, in fact, were to become one of the central themes of Chesnutt's life and work.

Charles's mother, North Carolinian Anne Maria Sampson Chesnutt, was headed west via wagon train in 1856 when she met Charles's father. A fellow native of Fayetteville, Andrew Chesnutt was also seeking a better life, away from the blatantly prejudiced pre–Civil War South.

Thousands of Ohioans, including many blacks and mulattoes, responded to Lincoln's 1861 call for volunteers. Among those who marched off to war with the state's famous Buckeye regiments was a Cleveland wagon master named Andrew Jackson Chesnutt. Because few units kept accurate records of their black "irregulars," historians have discovered frustratingly little about the military experiences of such men as Chesnutt. It can be assumed, however, that Chesnutt compiled a satisfactory service record; remaining in uniform all through the war, he was mustered out in 1865. At that point, he found himself near his hometown of Fayetteville, North Carolina, and he hastened off to visit his father.

Now old and ailing, Waddell Cade welcomed his son with joy, urging him to stay and send for his family. Postwar black emancipation had not ended

Members of Company E, Fourth U.S. Colored Infantry, line up for inspection in 1865. The soldiers were among the 179,000 blacks who, like Charles Chesnutt's father, volunteered to fight for the Union during the Civil War.

racism, but it had presented southern blacks with improved economic and educational opportunities. Cade offered to finance his son in the grocery business, and the young man accepted.

After setting up shop on Gillespie Street, Chesnutt wrote his wife and asked her to bring the three boys—Andrew, Jr., had been born shortly after his father's departure—back east. When she arrived, the five Chesnutts moved into their new home, another gift from Cade. Situated on its own C Street lot, the Chesnutt cottage stood behind a bank of cedar trees, a bit of local color that would one day serve Charles well. He and his brothers now began to explore the town their parents had once traveled hundreds of miles to escape.

In Fayetteville, as in many southern towns, blacks used the local black general store not only as a source of supplies but as a community center. Sooner or later, most of the town's black citizens—the educated and the unlettered, the sophisticated and the superstitious—showed up on the front porch of Andrew Chesnutt's store to trade ideas, news items, and gossip.

Charles worked in the store each afternoon and weekend, waiting on customers, stocking the shelves, and sweeping the floors. As he worked, he listened to the neighborly conversations that swirled around the store's broad wooden porch. At first unconsciously, later deliberately and painstakingly, he added everything he heard to the the private storehouse of impressions he would one day share with the rest of the world. Fayetteville was nurturing a writer.

Charles was growing up in a nation where a black writer could finally develop and even flourish. Under Reconstruction (the federal government's program to aid former slaves), the Freedmen's Bureau had established schools for black children across the South. Primitive when compared to facilities for

At the Civil War's close in 1865, General Oliver Otis Howard became commissioner of the Bureau of Refugees, Freedmen, and Abandoned Lands, a federal agency that constructed scores of black southern schools. Among the commissioner's legacies was the Howard School in Fayetteville, North Carolina, where Chesnutt both studied and taught.

Farmers and their produce-laden wagons assemble at Fayetteville's Market Square in the late 1860s. It was here, in the center of this sleepy southern community, that young Chesnutt saw his first example of racial violence: the body of a local black man murdered by white racists.

white children, the black schools nevertheless offered literacy and learning to youngsters who were willing to study. Charles was a star pupil at Fayetteville's Howard School, which had been named for General Oliver Otis Howard, commissioner of the Freedmen's Bureau and cofounder of Howard University, the outstanding black institution in Washington, D.C.

When he was not going to school or working in the store, Charles helped his mother with the younger children—two daughters, Clara and Mary, had arrived since the family's return to North Carolina—or did what he liked most in the world: reading. He read everything he could get his hands on. Fayetteville boasted its own bookstore, whose white proprietor, George Haigh, allowed Charles to browse to his heart's content. The bookseller undoubtedly liked the boy, but he was also practicing good business: Charles spent most of what he earned in the grocery store on books.

But nothing he read could have prepared Charles
for what he saw on the courthouse steps one day
in 1867. On that sunny Saturday morning, he was
working in the store as usual when he heard shouting
in the street; running outside, he found a crowd of
people talking excitedly and craning their necks
toward the building's wide marble staircase. Nine-
year-old Charles moved closer, then froze in horror:
On the steps lay the bleeding, bullet-riddled body of
a black man. The killers, three white men who
claimed their victim had raped a white woman, had
gunned him down in broad daylight in the middle
of town.

The three men were tried by a Union Army
court, which found them guilty and sentenced them
to death. A year later, however, the president of
the United States, North Carolina native Andrew
Johnson, pardoned all three. Young Charles filed the
incident away; many years later, this grim miscarriage
of justice would find its way into a memorable work
of fiction.

Four years after the Fayetteville murder, Charles
experienced another shock, this one not only deep
but personal. In 1871, Anne Maria Chesnutt gave
birth to her third daughter, Lillian; afterward, Anne
Maria sank into a coma and never recovered. Her
mother, Chloe, had already moved back from Cleveland to be closer to her daughter and grand-children.
Chloe did her best to raise the six motherless boys
and girls, but she found the never-ending job too
much for a woman her age.

Chloe wrote to her niece, Mary Ochiltree, an
18-year-old country girl who had never lived close to
a school. If Mary would come to Fayetteville and help
with the Chesnutt children, said Chloe, the young
woman could go to the Howard School. Delighted
by the prospect, Mary accepted quickly. As time
passed, the Chesnutt children grew to love her—and

At the age of 16, a solemn, conservatively dressed Charles Chesnutt embarked on his career as a teacher. His first job, in Charlotte, North Carolina, put him in charge of students bigger and older than he was, but he managed to gain both their respect and that of the school's principal, Cicero Harris.

so did their father. Within a year, Andrew Chesnutt and Mary Ochiltree were husband and wife.

Married or not, Mary Chesnutt had no intention of quitting school; along with her new stepchildren, she continued to attend Howard. Charles, too, genuinely loved school. Addicted to books, he also shone in composition and history, and he basked in the praise of his teachers, especially Howard's distinguished black principal, Robert Harris. By the time Charles was 14, however, his father said it was time for him to take a full-time job. Andrew and Mary Chesnutt had begun having children of their own, and the family needed all the money its members could earn.

Dutifully but sadly, Charles left Howard and went to work for a friend of his father's, a Fayetteville saloon keeper. The arrangement seemed satisfactory—until Robert Harris heard about it. When the school principal learned that his best student had quit his studies to work in a saloon, he stepped in quickly. Charles was soon earning a modest salary as a student teacher at the Howard School.

But more changes were in the air for the Chesnutts. In about 1872, Andrew Chesnutt's grocery store went bankrupt, partly because its trusting proprietor had extended too much credit to his customers. The family moved once more, this time to a farm two miles outside Fayetteville. Andrew worked hard, and his older children put in long hours after school, but the land was poor and produced little. For a while, Charles tried his hand at selling housewares door-to-door, but this, too, proved unprofitable. Money was still in short supply.

Once more, Robert Harris interceded, this time by finding Charles a good job: He would become an assistant to Harris's brother Cicero, a school principal in Charlotte, North Carolina. The work, which would place Charles in charge of boys and girls older than himself, would be challenging. Fortunately, Cicero Harris, like his brother Robert, proved to be intelligent, kind, and sensitive. He and his wife got along well with Charles, whom they supplied with a room in their own comfortable house. During school terms for the next three years, from 1873 until 1876, Charles and his boss taught together, ate together, and shared a home.

In June 1874, at the end of his first school year in Charlotte, the 16-year-old teacher went looking for a summer job. He hoped to find a post in one of the outlying rural districts where school lasted for only 10 weeks per year. Hearing about a possible opening in a Gaston County school, he walked 23 miles to apply for it. The county school director thanked him for his interest, but said the district had run out of money and could afford no classes at all that year.

Undiscouraged, Chesnutt next hiked over to remote Mecklenburg County—only to learn that the district had used all its educational funds to build a new school and had no money left to pay a teacher. The young educator finally found work in a country school not far from Fayetteville, which enabled him to save money by living at home. During these years, Chesnutt turned over most of his salary to his family. In the fall of 1874, he managed to double that income by earning a teaching certificate, thus qualifying himself for the handsome sum of $40 per month.

In the hours when he was not teaching, Chesnutt could usually be found deep in a book. A lifelong reading addict, he was especially fond of fiction and drama. Along with William Shakespeare, his favorite writers included British novelists Henry Fielding (*Tom Jones*), William Thackeray (*Vanity Fair*), Sir Walter Scott (*Ivanhoe*), Tobias Smollett (*The Expedition of Humphry Clinker*), and Daniel Defoe (*Robinson Crusoe*). Later, in his own first novel, *The House Behind the Cedars*, Chesnutt would write of a character who "had read all the books, [who] had tasted of the fruit of the Tree of Knowledge." For that character, said his creator, "happiness lay far beyond the sphere where he was born."

In the summer of 1874, Chesnutt decided to broaden his horizon by reading works on history, mathematics, Latin, and teaching. He also took organ lessons, practicing on the instrument at the home of his friend and mentor, Robert Harris. This went on until the fall, when he went back to Charlotte to work with Cicero Harris.

The following summer, Chesnutt found work in a school near Spartanburg, South Carolina. Here, the people he met, perhaps jealous of the bookish young teacher, treated him coldly. Now he spent more time alone than ever, reading and developing a new pastime: writing. He began keeping a journal, noting what books he read and recording his hopes and dreams for the future. In the entry for July 16, 1875, he wrote:

> I've been reading [poet Lord] Byron and [poet William] Cowper today. Cowper's *Task* [1783; a long poem in blank verse] is splendid. I will build a castle in the air. Cowper gives me the material in his *Task*. I don't wish my castle to be realized when I am old and worn out, but I would delight to lead a life like the one he describes in *The Garden*.
>
> Domestic happiness, thou only bliss
> Of Paradise which has survived the fall.
>
> I would wish my life to be like that—rural retirement, plenty to occupy the mind and hands, a dear companion to share my joys, a happy family growing up around me, and when having had enough of the world, I pass away to a better, "My children shall rise up and call me blessed" and I be regretted and remembered with love and respect by all who knew me. This is enjoying life! I believe that life was given to us to enjoy, and if God will help me, I intend to enjoy mine.

In his journal, Chesnutt began to consider many themes that would later appear in his published work.

During their first married years, Charles Chesnutt and his wife, Susan Perry Chesnutt, shared this Fayetteville house with Susan's parents. Her father, Edwin Perry, owned the Fayetteville Hotel Barber Shop, a favorite gathering place of the town's white male elite.

Of ongoing interest to the light-skinned young black man was color, its shades and its meaning. In the summer after he turned 17, for example, he wrote:

> One old fellow said today, "Look here, Tom. Here's a black as white as you are." . . . Twice today, or oftener, I have been taken for "white." At the pond this morning one fellow said he'd "be damned if there was any nigger blood in me." At Coleman's I passed.

By *passed*, of course, Chesnutt meant that he had entered an area—in this case Coleman's department store in Spartanburg—ordinarily off-limits to blacks. The importance that people of both races attached to skin color fascinated him, and he would later devote a significant portion of his writing to it.

In 1877, Chesnutt received a tempting offer: a teaching job at a brand-new college in Fayetteville, the State Colored Normal School of North Carolina. Specifically designed to train teachers for work in the area's black schools, the new institution would be headed by Chesnutt's mentor, Robert Harris. Promising a higher salary than the one Chesnutt had been getting in Charlotte, it was an offer impossible to turn down. Chesnutt, then 19 years old, accepted it and moved back to Fayetteville.

At first, he was as much of a loner as ever, spending all his free time with his books. With the rare exception of such people as bookseller George Haigh and the Harris brothers, Chesnutt knew no one—certainly no woman—who shared his interests in literature, philosophy, or sociology. "Home folks," he sadly told his journal, "cannot appreciate my talents, cannot understand my studies, nor enter into my feelings." Then he met Susan Perry.

Daughter of Edwin Perry, prosperous owner of the Fayetteville Hotel Barber Shop, Susan worked as a teacher at the Howard School. Charles was bookish, intellectual, reserved. Susan was bookish, intelligent, and full of empathy and admiration for her fellow

RE-CONSTRUCTION,
OR "A WHITE MAN'S GOVERNMENT".

teacher. Not surprisingly, the young instructors began spending most of their off-duty time together; also not surprisingly, they fell in love. On June 6, 1878, Susan Perry married Charles Chesnutt. The couple set up housekeeping in two rooms of Edwin Perry's house. A year later, they became the proud parents of their first child, Ethel.

Chesnutt loved his wife and daughter; he liked his job, got along well with his father-in-law, and continued to enjoy his books and his journal. Still, something was missing. Slavery had ended nearly two decades earlier, but the sentiments that sprang from it lived on in Fayetteville. As a black man, Chesnutt was regarded as an inferior by whites, even those with only a fraction of his education or intelligence. "I would think very meanly of myself," he confided to

"Re-construction," an on-target post–Civil War cartoon, shows a black man offering to help his former master. "You go to thunder!" responds the drowning southerner. "Do you think I'll let an infernal Nigger take Me by the hand?" It was this dogged white resistance to interracial equality that drove Chesnutt and other gifted blacks from their southern homeland.

The Howard School building in Fayetteville housed both Chesnutt's elementary school and, on the second floor, the State Colored Normal School of North Carolina. The 19-year-old writer-to-be started teaching here in 1877.

his journal, "if I didn't consider myself better than most of the white men I have met."

On the other hand, as a mulatto, Chesnutt was regarded with suspicion and occasional jealousy by blacks with darker skin. Reflecting on the fact that, one Christmas, he and his wife had received almost no holiday invitations, he wrote: "I am neither fish, flesh, nor fowl—neither 'nigger,' white, nor 'buckrah.'" (*Buckrah*, sometimes spelled *bukra* or *backra*, is a West African word, originally applied by slaves to their white masters.) He was, continued Chesnutt, "too 'stuck-up' for the colored folks, and, of course, not recognized by the whites." Pondering a solution to his isolation, he added, "Now these things I imagine I would escape from, in some degree, if I lived in the North."

Chesnutt also wanted to expand his education, but he felt he had reached a dead end. The handful of people in Fayetteville who could teach him anything new were white, and few would deign to teach a black man. Determined to try his luck elsewhere, he began studying shorthand, "which I hope," he noted, "will enable me to secure a position on the staff of some good newspaper, and then—work, work, work!" On October 16, 1878, he wrote:

> I will go to the North, where, although the prejudice sticks, like a foul blot on the fair scutcheon of American liberty, yet a man may enjoy these privileges if he has the money to pay for them. I will live down the prejudice, I will crush it out. If I can exalt my race, if I can gain the applause of the good, and approbation of God, the thoughts of the ignorant and prejudiced will not concern me.

The following June, shortly after the school year ended, Chesnutt left Fayetteville for Washington, D.C.

3

"I WANT FAME"

CHARLES CHESNUTT ARRIVED in Washington, D.C., full of high hopes and lofty sentiments. He wanted to do nothing less than to "test the social problem," to find out if the American "myth of equality" was real. "I shall not undertake [the journey] for myself alone," he said, "but for my children, for the people with whom I am connected, for humanity!"

Chesnutt planned to find work as a stenographer (shorthand expert), then send for his wife and daughter. If he succeeded, he had no intention of returning to Fayetteville. Nevertheless, he signed on for another year at the Normal School in case anything went wrong in the nation's capital. Unfortunately, it did.

Washington taught the somewhat naive Chesnutt some hard lessons. "Employment-seeking in a strange place, even with the best of qualifications," he discovered, "is a weary work." He also discovered that an expensive big city offers few joys to a poor man. He decided, in fact, that poverty was an even greater barrier to success than color. "I have learned," he wrote, sounding like the wide-eyed country boy he was, "that to live in a large city requires considerable money." After enduring weeks of loneliness and frustration, and meeting no luck in finding a job, he concluded that "the advantages of city life can only be fully enjoyed by the wealthy" and went home.

Brimming with optimism, Chesnutt went to seek his fortune in Washington, D.C., in the summer of 1879; unable to find a job, he returned to Fayetteville that fall. "Employment-seeking in a strange place is a weary work," the young teacher said afterward, but the trip "enlarged my experience and knowledge of the world."

33

Chesnutt, who liked to take a positive view of life, firmly told himself that his sojourn in the capital had been productive. He recorded his view of the trip in his journal:

> The visit to the Art Gallery, studios, schools, museums, etc. . . . have enlarged my experience and knowledge of the world; and by robbing it of some of the stage effects of distance and imagination, have made me better content to remain at home and work faithfully in my present sphere of usefulness.

A year after Chesnutt's return to Fayetteville, in the fall of 1880, Robert Harris died. The young man grieved for his friend but was heartened to learn that before his death Harris had recommended Chesnutt as his successor. Thus, at the age of 22, Chesnutt became principal of the Normal School, earning the impressive salary of $75 a month. The family's new-found prosperity enabled them to move out of the Perry residence and into a house of their own, now a necessity. Ethel was already a year old, and a new baby—who would turn out to be daughter Helen—was on the way.

For many men, particularly a black man of the 1880s, Chesnutt's accomplishments might have seemed enough for a lifetime. He held a prestigious job, owned his own home, headed a fine family, and had time to do the things he loved. He continued to spend hours reading fiction, nonfiction, and plays; he attended lectures; he gave lessons in organ, voice, and Latin; he kept up with his shorthand practice; and he never stopped writing in his journal. Still, he frankly admitted (if only to himself), he wanted more.

"I want fame," he wrote. "I want money; I want to raise my children in a different rank of life from that I sprang from." Teaching, he knew, even with "all the economy and prudence and parsimony in the world," would never make him wealthy. And "in law

The arrival of Ethel, the Chesnutts' first child, made her young father concentrate harder than ever on improving his prospects. "I want money," he told his journal. "I want to raise my children in a different rank of life from that which I sprang from."

or medicine," he figured, "I would be compelled to wait half a lifetime to accomplish anything."

Chesnutt decided that there was only one route to his goals: literature. Writing, he said, "is the only thing I can do without capital [money to invest] under my present circumstances, except teach." Convinced that "literature pays the successful," he laid out his 1881 blueprint for the future: "I shall strike for an entering wedge in the literary world."

Perhaps the strongest influence in Chesnutt's new approach to his life was a white man he had never met. In 1880, Albion W. Tourgée had written a novel called *Fool's Errand.* An instant best-seller, the book earned critical raves and brought its author $20,000 plus ongoing royalty payments. The story of Tourgée's success made Chesnutt's mouth water.

Fool's Errand offered a portrait of black southern life, a subject that many whites, especially in the North, seemed to find fascinating. ("Men are always more ready to extend their sympathy to those at a distance than to the suffering ones in their midst,"

Chesnutt noted wryly.) If a white writer could create a good novel about blacks, he reasoned, a black writer could surely write a great novel on the subject. "I think I must write a book," he confided to his journal.

All his life, Chesnutt had kept mental notes on his experiences, vaguely thinking that he might one day organize this material into fiction. Now he began to keep formal notes. He would, he told his journal, "record my impressions of men and things, and such incidents or conversations which take place within my knowledge, with a view to future use in literary work." He began keeping a separate file entitled "Ideas for Future Use," which included such entries as "Aunt Henrietta Wright—preaching—organ— prayers—begging," and "The wonderful conversion of Uncle Isham from Episcopacy to Methodism."

Chesnutt's purpose in writing, he said, would be less for the betterment of blacks than for the betterment of whites. Calling racism "a barrier to the moral progress of the American people," he said rather grandly, "I would be one of the first to head a determined, organized crusade against it."

To make it as a writer, Chesnutt decided he would have to leave the South. He had another reason, too, for moving north: He wanted his children to escape the South's pervasive racial prejudice. His stenographic skills were now awesome, thanks in part to his wife; night after night, she read aloud and he took down the words, constantly improving his speed. By 1883, he could take shorthand at the astonishing rate of 200 words per minute. Now, surely, he could earn enough to live comfortably while he readied himself for his real mission: to aid not only his own family but the rest of his race.

When Chesnutt announced his plans to head north a second time, some friends and relatives approved, but many, including his father, thought him foolish. Why, they asked, would he give up his home and well-established career to go to a strange land where he had no job at all? After all, they pointed out, he had tried and failed once already. But Chesnutt was determined to make his mark on the world. In the spring of 1883, he resigned as principal of the Normal School, bid a final farewell to Fayetteville, and boarded a train for New York City.

His stay in Manhattan proved more fruitful than his Washington, D.C., venture: He soon found himself a good job as a Wall Street columnist, spent six months building up his skills and self-confidence, and earned enough to establish his family in the city of his final choice, Cleveland, Ohio.

Once he was settled in the Midwest, Chesnutt set about building a career. Starting in the accounting department of the Nickel Plate Railroad Company, he quickly gained promotion to the company's legal department, then took a job as a stenographer in the office of a white judge, Samuel Williamson. While he was there, he studied law on his own.

In his off-hours, Chesnutt wrote short stories and essays about the world around him. A perfectionist, he was rarely satisfied with his own work

New Yorkers sedately drive along Fifth Avenue, past St. Patrick's Cathedral, in the 1880s. Moving to the city in 1883, Chesnutt quickly became a newspaperman, worked for a few months, then moved to Ohio. Rowdy Manhattan, he thought, was no place to bring up children.

Choo-Choo Mail Pouch, urges a brand-new, electrified 1902 chewing-tobacco ad in Cleveland, Ohio. Born in the city in 1858, Chesnutt returned to the bustling, modern metropolis in 1883. He stayed for the rest of his life.

and often wrote, revised, completed, then threw away his pieces. But his desire to write was constant, and each time he thought he had failed, he would begin again. He regarded even the tossed-out manuscripts as useful, because they had supplied him with practice, and, he hoped, brought him closer to the day when his work would see publication.

That day came in 1885, thanks to the literary taste of Samuel Sidney McClure, an Irish-born editor and publisher. S. S. McClure had begun a small publishing revolution the year before, when he established the first American newspaper syndicate. Syndicates, which today sell and distribute most of the comic strips, editorial cartoons, and opinion columns that appear in the nation's newspapers, began when McClure conceived the idea of buying the rights to new short stories and articles and then selling them to papers around the country for simultaneous publication.

To publicize the new McClure Syndicate, its owner announced a story contest and offered a prize. As soon as he read about the contest, Chesnutt fired off one of the few pieces that had escaped his trash basket, a short story called "Uncle Peter's House." It failed to win the contest, but McClure liked it, paid Chesnutt $10 for it, and sold it to the *Cleveland News and Herald*, which ran it in December 1885. Charles Chesnutt, 27 years old, had finally broken into print.

The publication of "Uncle Peter's House" was more than a breakthrough for Chesnutt; it marked the first occasion when conventional fiction showed post–Civil War southern blacks as human beings of worth and dignity. Until this point, black characters had appeared only in the "dialect stories" of such popular white authors as Thomas Nelson Page (*In Ole Virginia*) and Joel Chandler Harris (the Uncle Remus series).

In these authors' works, blacks were of two types: comically uneducable but lovable and loyal retainers to their former "massas," or lazy, gin-guzzling, razor-wielding rascals. At his worst, a black was barbaric or uppity; a "good Negro" might be careless, but he knew "his place" and was usually happy, unfailingly faithful, and always hilarious.

Chesnutt's "Uncle Peter" is a complete departure from these stereotypes. A former slave who lives in postwar North Carolina, Peter has always dreamed of buying his own land and building his own home. Although saddled by poverty and unjust debt, he acquires a small plot and starts digging and planting. The land turns out to be too poor for crops, and Peter is subjected to terrifying visits from the Ku Klux Klan, whose members consider him "radical." It begins to seem as if he will never reach his goal, but Peter does not falter.

Chesnutt gave Peter the kind of virtues that the era's fiction writers usually reserved for white charac-

An illustration from a Joel Chandler Harris Uncle Remus tale shows Br'er Fox chatting with the Tar Baby. Harris's popular stories had literary merit, but their stereotyped black characters—invariably kind, patient, and none too bright—had little basis in reality. Chesnutt, on the other hand, wrote about people as they were; his short story "Uncle Peter's House," for example, centered on a character who was intelligent, industrious, responsible, sensitive, and black.

ters: The former field hand is sober, hardworking, philosophical about injustice, and deeply religious. Peter never finishes building his house, but as he lies dying, he makes his son promise to complete the job, and the reader is sure the boy will follow the brave old man's wishes.

"Uncle Peter's House" is a moving story, accurately depicting two major aspects of postwar black life in the South: the hard conditions that faced blacks and the strong religious faith that helped many survive slavery and much ill treatment after it. More important, the story made American literary history by presenting a black as an upstanding, sympathetic human being, a man who would be a "credit" to any race.

During the next three years, the McClure Syndicate published seven more Chesnutt stories: "A Tight Boot," "A Bad Night," "Two Wives," "A Secret Ally," "A Midnight Adventure," "A Doubtful Success," and "Cartwright's Mistake." Some of the stories, such as "A Tight Boot," reflect the misery of slavery, while others, like the hilarious "A Bad Night," deal with the mishaps of everyday life.

During this period, Chesnutt also wrote poems, some of which he published in the *Cleveland Voice*. He sold stories to *Family Fiction* and to *The Great International Weekly Story Paper* and wrote humorous sketches for the magazines *Tid-Bits* and *Puck*. Chesnutt often set these sketches in business offices peopled by the kind of lawyers and railroad men he had come to know at work.

In March 1887, Chesnutt, the self-taught lawyer, took the Ohio bar examination (the test each state requires of anyone who wants to practice law in that state). As he had anticipated, he passed the exam, and to his pleased surprise, he also earned the highest score of that year. Now he could think about starting a law practice. He was deciding which way to proceed when his employer, Judge Samuel Williamson, gave him some fatherly counsel.

Even as an educated man living in the North, observed Williamson, Chesnutt would find it hard to overcome prejudice against blacks. He suggested that the young man take his family to Europe, where racism rarely showed its malevolent face. Chesnutt listened carefully, thanked the judge for his advice, then went home to discuss it with his wife.

In the end, the Chesnutts agreed that the real test—and perhaps the greater triumph—would come from achieving success where the odds were the toughest. They remained in Cleveland. Law degree in hand, Chesnutt moved into the prestigious law office of Henderson, Kline, and Tolles, where he worked as a stenographer, waited for business as an attorney, and continued to dream of his future as a writer.

Two comedians, one of them in blackface, perform in the early 1890s. In this era, when Chesnutt started writing and publishing his "color-line" fiction, real blacks rarely appeared before white audiences; "darkies"—always grinning, clumsy, and hilariously stupid—were played by white actors.

4

CONJURING UP A BOOK

I N THE SUMMER of 1887, the *Atlantic Monthly*—then as today, one of the nation's major literary magazines—accepted Charles Chesnutt's "The Goophered Grapevine." It was the first of what would come to be known as Chesnutt's "conjure" stories, a group of southern tales told in southern black dialect and involving spells and witchcraft. Chestnutt published a second conjure story, "Po' Sandy," in the *Atlantic* in May 1888. Another, the spooky "The Conjurer's Revenge," appeared in 1889.

All these stories feature John, a transplanted white Yankee, John's wife, and a mulatto former slave named Uncle Julius McAdoo; in each, Julius tells John of the old plantation days, when strange and wonderful things happened as a result of ancient African sorcery. As the tales unwind, the reader comes to see that John is not as wise and worldly as he thinks he is, and that Julius is far more practical and sophisticated than he looks.

Chesnutt's work was now reaching a larger audience. Among his new admirers was George Washington Cable, a well-known white author (*The Cavalier, Old Creole Days*) and social reformer. A former cavalryman in the Confederate army, Cable had become a controversial figure in the South, where he wrote and lectured on behalf of black

Light-skinned and blue-eyed, Chesnutt could have ignored his black ancestry, but he never considered it. He believed that blacks should improve their lot not by "passing" but by achieving political and social equality: "People who can . . . feel that they are men and women and free citizens do not drag their dull way through life like fettered slaves," he said. "The slaves of a generation ago," he added, "will contribute their full share to the future greatness of the nation and of humanity."

Slaves trade stories outside a plantation cabin in the 1850s. The folk tales and legends of Africa, repeated by each generation to the next, formed the basis of Chesnutt's first book, The Conjure Woman, *a collection of "conjure" tales that deal with ancient sorcery and witchcraft.*

rights. He also managed the *Open Letter Club*, a publication that served as a forum for different views of the South's "race problem."

Much impressed with "The Goophered Grapevine" and "Po' Sandy," Cable wrote a congratulatory letter to Chesnutt. The two writers began corresponding regularly, and Chesnutt soon volunteered to work for the *Open Letter Club* by finding contributors, collecting material, and typing manuscripts.

In 1889, Chesnutt started expressing some of his own views on the southern "problem." His first serious essay, "An Inside View of the Negro Question," defined the obstacles standing between black people and full U.S. citizenship. In this piece, Chesnutt made the realistic but shocking suggestion that if American society continued to deny equality to its black citizens, the whole country would pay the price. "The republic shall be menaced," he warned, "by the presence within its borders of a large and increasing portion of its population who have no share in its glory and no respect for its institutions."

Cable, who had advised Chesnutt on the writing of the essay, also tried to help him publish it. But the piece was a political hot potato; despite Cable's celebrity, the *Century*, *Forum*, and *North American Review* refused to touch it. "'An Inside View of the Negro Question,'" said the *Century's* editor in a curiously worded rejection letter, "[is] so timely and political . . . that we cannot handle it."

Chesnutt had better luck with his second essay: "What Is a White Man?" appeared in the New York *Independent* in 1889. The piece discussed the definition of race, which all the southern states dealt with differently.

The Mississippi code of 1885 stated that anyone with more than one-fourth black blood was black. In Georgia, a person with *any* black ancestry was legally black. In South Carolina, the law stated that when a person's color was unclear, a jury must decide it after considering reputation and status: If the questionable individual was judged to be "good," he or she was white. All told, these laws were intended to make enforcement of segregation easier and to prevent marriages between blacks and whites.

Chesnutt attacked the "manifest absurdity" of this classification system in "What Is a White Man?" If a man is "fifteen-sixteenths white," he asked, how could he be defined as black? Not only were these laws offensive and demeaning to people of color, he maintained, they were unenforceable. And, noting that the laws had been written to protect "Anglo-Saxon racial purity," he pointedly suggested that purity might be better protected by the practice of virtue and morality.

In the same essay, Chesnutt tackled an issue that had always personally distressed him. Although his parents had been married, his grandparents, Ann Chesnutt and Waddell Cade, had not. Because they had been legally forbidden to wed, their children bore the stigma of illegitimacy, a heavy burden in that era, particularly in the South.

Charles Chesnutt had bitterly resented society's assumption that he—and every "colored man or woman whose complexion is white or nearly white"—was "presumed . . . to be the offspring of a union not sanctified by law." This might once have been the case, he continued, "but the times have changed." With this essay, Chesnutt became known as a spokesman for black people's concerns as well as a storyteller.

Surprisingly, it was as a storyteller that Chesnutt experienced the deepest frustration. The public, he told Cable, expected black characters to resemble Joel Chandler Harris's popular Uncle Remus, the resourceful, loyal, sweet-tempered slave. The "chief virtues" of such characters, said Chesnutt, "have been their doglike fidelity to their old masters, for whom they have been willing to sacrifice almost life itself. Such characters exist. . . . But I can't write about these people, or rather I won't write about them."

"Ah! my dear Miss Snowball," gushes a white man to his beaming black companion, "we have at last reached our political and social paradise." Published in 1864, this cartoon reflected an opinion—that interracial marriage would destroy society—common among 19th-century whites. Chesnutt objected to such thinking; he never advocated intermarriage, but he believed that laws against it insulted both races.

Chesnutt also despised another group of popularized fictional blacks: "cultivated white Negroes [who] are always bewailing their fate and cursing the drop of black blood which 'taints'—I hate the word, it implies corruption—their otherwise pure race." In an 1890 letter to Cable, Chesnutt expanded on his literary grievances:

> The kind of stuff I could write, if I were not all the time oppressed by a fear that this line or this sentiment would offend somebody's prejudices, jar on somebody's American-trained sense of propriety, would . . . [be that] in which Negroes, and "Coloured People" play either principal or subordinate parts. They [would] figure as lawyers, as doctors, as musicians, as authors, as judges, as people of wealth and station. They [would] love and . . . marry without reference to their race. . . . [There would be] nothing extraordinary in a talented well-bred colored man, nothing amorphous in a pretty gentle-spirited colored girl.

Meanwhile, Chesnutt's fiction continued to appear in the *Atlantic Monthly*, the *Overland Review*, and other magazines. Among the stories he published in 1889 was "The Sheriff's Children." An example of the "kind of stuff" he liked to write, this tale appeared in the *Independent* and is a daring piece of writing that focuses on the tragic fate of a young mulatto and his father, a white southern aristocrat.

This story is of particular interest because it illustrates a theme Chesnutt used again and again: The sins of the fathers—in this case, the slaveholding Old South—are always visited on the children—the New South, which includes free blacks. Set in a sleepy postwar southern town, "The Sheriff's Children" tells the story of a former planter who once impregnated a slave, then escaped all responsibility by selling both the woman and the child.

As the tale opens, the planter, now sheriff of the town, saves a young black murder suspect from being lynched by a white mob. Now the sheriff's prisoner,

Joel Chandler Harris's popular Uncle Remus entertains his young "massa" with a tale. The "doglike fidelity" of Remus and other such characters left Chesnutt cold. "I can't write about these people," he told a friend, "or rather I won't write about them."

Beaded curtains—standard in well-furnished Victorian homes— fill the doorway leading to Chesnutt's study, part of the new house he bought in 1889. The author created most of his important work by the light of the gas lamp (center) on his highly polished wooden desk.

the young man reveals that he is also his natural son. But, he asks bitterly, "What father's duty have you ever performed for me?" He is about to kill his father and escape, when his half sister shoots him. She and her father bandage the young man, but during the night he deliberately rips off the bandage and bleeds to death.

As he looks down at his dead son, the sheriff becomes agonizingly aware that he cannot "shake off the consequences of his sin"; he must accept responsibility for his own acts. Likewise, Chesnutt seems to be saying, the white South must learn to admit and to atone for the monstrous moral crimes its ancestors committed against the black race.

Many years after he published "The Sheriff's Children," Chesnutt remarked that 1889 marked a turning point in his writing. From then on, he said, "substantially all" of his fiction dealt "with the problems of mixed blood." The year 1889 was important to Chesnutt in other ways, too. His family, now numbering five people (Edwin had been born in 1883), began to feel cramped in their snug little house on Wilcutt Avenue, and in May, they moved to a larger home at 64 Brenton Street. All the Chesnutts worked hard at fixing up the new place, which soon seemed as warm and inviting as the old one.

In the new house, as in the old, Charles Chesnutt devoted his evenings to the children. Each night before they went to bed, he read them his own childhood favorites: *Mother Goose*, *Alice in Wonderland*, *Gulliver's Travels*, and other classics. When the children had gone to sleep, Chesnutt turned to his own writing.

In 1889, that writing included a story longer than any he had done so far. In it he intended to examine attitudes about intermarriage and skin color—attitudes of blacks as well as of whites. In "The Sheriff's Children," he had started writing about the problems facing people of mixed blood; in this one, tentatively entitled "Rena," he would probe the issue even more deeply. He finished a draft of the story, then sent it to George Cable for his opinion.

The story was good, responded Cable, but not quite as good as it could be; he suggested that Chesnutt keep working on it. The writer followed his friend's advice, and in early 1890 he sent him the new version; Cable read it, liked it, and sent it on to Richard Watson Gilder, editor of the *Century* magazine.

Known as a tough but fair critic, Gilder applauded the writing but said he felt the "sentiment was amorphous": Chesnutt's point was unclear. Both Gilder and Cable suggested that Chesnutt rework the story yet again. And this was just the beginning: "Rena" would not see publication for another 10 years, and by then the story would have undergone some half-dozen further revisions as well as a name change.

Meanwhile, Chesnutt's own name was gaining modest fame, especially in his hometown. The slender, distinguished author-attorney-stenographer with his trademark bushy mustache and impeccable tailoring had become a fixture in Cleveland's upper-class black society. In the late 1880s, he and his wife received an invitation to join the Social Circle, the city's most exclusive black social group.

Established in 1869, the Circle was made up of well-to-do professional couples who gathered for periodic musical recitals, poetry readings, and literary discussions. (Thinly disguised under another name, the Social Circle would later appear in a Chesnutt story.) Most of the Circle's members were older than the Chesnutts; their three children, Ethel, Helen, and Edwin, were the only youngsters who appeared at the social group's Christmas parties and summer picnics.

By late 1890, however, the three young Chesnutts had to share their star billing with a fourth member. One December night, 10-year-old Helen suddenly woke up. Hearing what sounded like a plaintive wail from the family cat, she got out of bed and went downstairs. She found her father pacing back and forth, and asked him to help her find the cat. Giving his daughter a tiny smile, Chesnutt took her hand and led her to a corner, where the pet lay sleeping peacefully. Relieved, Helen returned to her bed. In the morning, to their amazed delight, the children found their mother cradling their brand-new baby sister.

Although Dorothy's arrival gave Chesnutt another mouth to feed, his court-reporting business supplied him with plenty of money to do it. He had started the stenography venture simply to keep afloat until his law practice began, but it had taken off quickly. By the time of Dorothy's birth, it was a flourishing business with a number of employees and a large clientele. Nevertheless, Chesnutt kept writing steadily.

In mid-1891, he sent a letter to Houghton Mifflin and Company, the Boston-based book publishing firm that owned the *Atlantic Monthly*. Noting that the company's magazine had published a number of his stories, he asked if Houghton Mifflin would be interested in publishing a book-length collection of his short works. He proposed including "Rena," the long story he had now rewritten several times, plus several other selections, some of which had already been published in magazines.

"There is one fact which would give this volume distinction," Chesnutt wrote. "It is the first contribution by an American of acknowledged African descent to purely imaginative literature." He said it was time for blacks to be given a chance to share their view of the world. "These people," he continued, "have not had their day in court. Their friends have written of them, and their enemies; but this is, so far as I know, the first instance where a writer with any of their blood has attempted a literary portrayal of them. If these stories have any merit, I think it is more owing to this new point of view than to any other thing."

Houghton Mifflin turned him down. The editors said they liked the stories, but that before such a collection would sell, Chesnutt would have to develop a wider reputation. They suggested he keep writing stories for another year or two, so the reading public could become more familiar with his work and style. Then, when the collection finally appeared, people would recognize the author's name and buy the book without hesitation.

Seeing his name on a book cover would take longer than Chesnutt had expected—and "Rena" had been rejected yet again. The writer was naturally disappointed, but he finally decided the Houghton Mifflin editors were probably right. Taking their advice, he kept on writing and publishing stories, and dreaming of becoming the nation's first black author of a book of fiction. ❧

5

CROSSING THE
COLOR LINE

❦

IN THE MID-1890s, Chesnutt's duties as a businessman, husband, and father kept him busy. His daughters Ethel and Helen, so close in age that they had started school together, entered their senior high school year in 1896. In another year, they would be ready to enter college, fulfilling their father's longtime dream. Poverty and racial prejudice had kept him out of college, but what he could not do, his children could. He looked forward to the day when they entered a fine university.

Then Ethel and Helen announced that they did not *want* to go to college. Their parents were shocked and puzzled. The family could afford to send them; both girls were doing well in their studies, and they lived in the North, where colleges routinely accepted highly qualified black students. What, Susan and Charles asked each other, could their daughters be thinking of?

After a little patient questioning, they got the answer. The sisters had been happy in Cleveland's integrated schools. As they got older, however, their white classmates began to avoid them; they no longer wished to associate with black girls on a social level. "After all," a white girlfriend had said one day, "you *are* Negroes." Then she explained what she meant: "Mother says that while it was all right for us to go

The three oldest Chesnutt children, Ethel, Edwin, and Helen, assume solemn expressions for a Cleveland photographer in the early 1890s. Happily ignorant of racial prejudice during early childhood, the girls met it with a jolt in high school, when a longtime girlfriend stopped seeing them. "After all," said the patronizing white girl, "you are Negroes."

together when we were younger, now that we are growing up, we must consider Society, and we just can't go together anymore."

Shortly afterward, this young woman appeared at the Chesnutts' door. Carrying an armload of books, she was ready to study with Ethel and Helen as usual. Susan Chesnutt, who had listened to her daughters' reports with sorrow and anger, quietly asked if the girl's mother knew where she was. Certainly, responded the girl cheerfully. Her mother said it was all right to study with Ethel and Helen as long as she did not mix with them in social situations.

For years, Susan Chesnutt had been feeding this girl milk and cookies, helping her with her homework, listening to her problems. Now she had turned into a total stranger, a young woman who thought herself better than her old friends. Susan Chesnutt picked up the girl's jacket and books and silently handed them to their owner. Then, with icy courtesy, she invited her to leave. And not to return.

Ethel and Helen listened to their usually gentle, soft-spoken mother with amazement—and new respect. They were beginning to understand that one person's boast of superiority over another meant nothing; it was merely a string of empty words that reflected no one but their speaker. Over the next few weeks, the family talked at length about racial prejudice, racial pride, individual potential, and personal accomplishment. With a renewed sense of self-worth, the Chesnutt girls applied to Smith, one of the finest women's colleges in the nation. The celebrated New England institution accepted them both, and in the fall of 1897, they proudly departed for Northampton, Massachusetts.

In the same year, Chesnutt sent three new stories to the *Atlantic*, which accepted two—"The Wife of His Youth" and "The March of Progress"—for publication. (They appeared a year later, in the summer of 1898.) Like the rest of the author's "color-line" stories, these two deal with the life of mulattoes who look white but are legally black.

"The Wife of His Youth" is set in Groveland, a fictional version of Cleveland, and features a social club nicknamed the Blue Vein Society. This organization, which bears a strong resemblance to the Chesnutts' own club, the Cleveland Social Circle, admits no one but those with skin "white enough to show blue veins." "The Wife of His Youth" is the story of Mr. Ryder, a former slave who has become a leading member of Groveland's black community; he is "the dean of the Blue Veins."

Ryder intends to marry Molly Dixon, a beautiful, well-educated young widow with very pale skin; to announce his engagement, he invites his friends to a party. Then his past steps forward to claim him: His "plantation wife," Liza Jane—the older woman to whom he was unofficially married during long-ago slavery days—suddenly reappears. Ryder is torn. Molly represents "the upward process of absorption"—everything "he had been wishing and waiting for." Liza Jane, whom Ryder had believed dead, represents a "backward step": Devoted, humble, and generous of spirit, she is also elderly, illiterate, and very black.

In the end, Ryder takes Liza Jane's hand and introduces her to the crowd as his wife, thereby illustrating Chesnutt's argument that honor and good character far outweigh prestige and pale skin. "The Wife of His Youth," in fact, illustrates the main themes of all Chesnutt's "color-line" fiction. As he saw it, the color line presented a major problem for virtually all Americans—blacks, whites, and people of mixed race. He believed that solving the problem was "a matter primarily of individual effort, of the exercise of moral force."

An illustration from The Wife of His Youth and Other Stories of the Color Line, *published in 1899, shows Mr. Ryder and his wife, Liza Jane, at a meeting of Ryder's social club. In the story, Ryder has told club members an account of a successful light-skinned black man whose black, almost forgotten plantation wife reappears; in the picture, he is saying, "This is the woman, and I am the man."*

To help destroy racial prejudice, Chesnutt used his fiction to attack racial stereotypes. Most popular fiction of the day, he asserted, offered readers five types of "Negro characters," none of them realistic, all of them dangerous. First, he said, there was "the bad Negro," the agitator or lawbreaker. Then there was "the good Negro," who loyally served whites. Next came "the modern 'white man's nigger'—a preacher or politician who said the things whites liked to hear. Fourth and fifth were "the wastrel type" (defined by Chesnutt as a person who "squandered his substance in riotous living"); and "the minstrel type," a man who "tried to keep white folks in good humor by his capers and antics."

Although "The Wife of His Youth" satirizes the snobbishness and prejudice that Chesnutt had observed among light-skinned blacks, it is also sympathetic toward its characters. "I shared their sentiments to a degree," remarked Chesnutt later, "though I could see the comic side of them."

"The March of Progress," the second of Chesnutt's 1898 *Atlantic* stories, is set in the fictional southern town of Patesville (Fayetteville) in the 1880s. The town's black school board must make a decision: whether to rehire Miss Noble or replace her with Mr. Williams. Noble, an elderly white northerner who has dedicated her life to Patesville's black community, has taught its children and served as its nurse, preacher, and defender. She not only wants to keep her job; she needs it.

Williams, however, also has a powerful claim on the position. A young black resident of the town who has recently graduated from college, he is seen by some of the school board members as representing the "march of progress" of the South's blacks. "Self-preservation is the first law of nature," these members assert; "the race must stand together." Eventually, however, the board decides moral responsibility must outweigh racial bonds, and it rehires Noble.

"The March of Progress" is pure vintage Chesnutt, in that it contains perhaps the single most important element in his work: the idea that before true progress can be made—by any group of people— racial consciousness, black or white, must disappear. Success, says Chesnutt, cannot be defined by economic or social superiority; it can be measured only in terms of *moral* superiority.

A few critics complained that Chesnutt spoiled "The March of Progress" by tacking on a melodramatic and too-convenient ending: Miss Noble dies, and Mr. Williams gets the job after all. Nevertheless, "The March of Progress" raises hard questions about loyalty and where it belongs, and it marks a new level of sophistication in Chesnutt's work.

Overall, both "March" and "Wife" received high praise from most critics and general readers. Editor and novelist William Dean Howells, the era's most influential literary figure (*The Rise of Silas Lapham, The Quality of Mercy*), called Chesnutt "one of the superior short-story writers in America."

Pleased as he was by these stories' popularity, Chesnutt was still determined to publish a book. He next began working on "A Business Career," a long story about a pair of white office associates who fall in love, which he was thinking about expanding into a novel. Was he now famous enough, he wondered, to sell a book of stories?

In early 1898, he wrote to Walter Hines Page, editor of the *Atlantic* as well as a Houghton Mifflin director. Page had once spoken encouragingly about the possibility of a Chesnutt short-story collection; now the author sent him the first draft of "A Business Career" and asked if he would like to publish it as a novel or, perhaps, as one of a book-length collection.

Walter Hines Page, Chesnutt's editor and literary adviser, enters New York harbor aboard an ocean liner in 1916. A longtime publishing executive, Page also served as American ambassador to Great Britain from 1913 to 1918.

Chesnutt also enclosed a large selection of his other work, including the three "conjure" stories: "The Goophered Grapevine," "Po' Sandy," and "The Conjurer's Revenge."

Page's response started on a discouraging note. The field of publishing, he said, was "absolutely over-crowded with novels." To justify the expense of publication, a new novel would have to be exceptional, which, in his opinion, "A Business Career" was not. Furthermore, Houghton Mifflin was still doubtful about the sales potential of a short-story collection: "The public," said Page, "seems thoroughly to have made up its mind that the business of the short story is completely done when it appears in a magazine."

Saving the good news until the end, Page said he really liked the "conjure" stories. If Chesnutt had enough of them "to make a book," he added, there was "a possibility of Mssrs. Houghton Mifflin and Company's doing something for you." At this point, Chesnutt thought he was through with writing dialect stories about "the realm of superstition"; he much preferred what he called "the region of feeling and passion"—the color-line pieces that addressed the issues he cared about. But he was almost 40 years old, and he wanted his name on a book. It seemed to be now or never. Setting to work at once, he produced six new conjure stories in six weeks.

Page was satisfied. In the fall of 1898, he wrote Chesnutt a formal note of acceptance: "It gives us great pleasure to report that after thorough consideration we feel disposed to publish your collection of short stories." He went on to say that, if Chesnutt approved, he would use the original three conjure tales plus four of the new ones: "Mars Jeems's Nightmare," "Sis Becky's Pickaninny," "The Gray Wolf's Ha'nt," and "Hot-Foot Hannibal." The author agreed with the editor. In March 1899, Houghton Mifflin published *The Conjure Woman* by 40-year-old Charles W. Chesnutt.

Four months later, Chesnutt traveled to Boston to talk to Page. He had already written him about the possibility of publishing another book of stories, and he now delivered a complete manuscript for review. After promising to read it quickly, Page introduced the author to a visiting friend, M. A. DeWolfe Howe, editor of the *Beacon Biographies*, a series of short books for young people about eminent Americans.

Literary Bostonians check out a window display at the Old Corner Bookstore, a landmark of the city's publishing hub. Visiting the area in 1899, Chesnutt persuaded Walter Page to publish a second collection of his short fiction: The Wife of His Youth and Other Stories of the Color Line.

Howe told Chesnutt he was planning a book about Frederick Douglass, the great black abolitionist, orator, and author who had died four years earlier. Chesnutt had heard Douglass speak and had long admired him; he soon found himself agreeing to write the biography. Howe asked for a completed manuscript in 10 weeks, which Chesnutt promised to—and did—deliver. "It is a new line for me," he told Page, "but . . . I think I shall do very well with it."

Before Chesnutt left, Page asked him for a favor. He was scheduled to give a lecture at Greenacre, a summer school in Eliot, Maine, but was unable to make the trip. Would Chesnutt substitute for him? The annual lectures always attracted prominent people, said Page, and Chesnutt's appearance would be good advertising for his books. The author, who had given occasional lectures in Cleveland, agreed to do it. At Greenacre, he addressed what he later called "quite an audience of highly intellectual people" about the problems faced by blacks in the South. He wrote to Page about the event:

> I frankly confessed my lack of skill as a platform speaker, but they were good enough to say I underestimated my effort, and that any lack of rhetorical graces was more than compensated for by my evident knowledge of the subject and the interesting nature of what I said. . . . I am afraid I

dwelt more on the political and civil status of Negroes in the South and didn't have time to properly consider the remedies.

I did suggest education, however, as the most obvious and immediate palliative, but maintained that race troubles would never cease until the constitutional amendments were strictly observed, in the spirit in which they were meant, the color line entirely wiped out before the law, and equal justice and equal opportunity extended to every man in every relation in life. This sentiment was vigorously applauded.

A month after his return to Cleveland, Chesnutt learned that Houghton Mifflin had accepted his second book, which Page planned to release under the title *The Wife of His Youth and Other Stories of the Color Line*. Chesnutt must have smiled at the irony: After vainly trying for a decade to get one book published, he would now have three in one year: *The Conjure Woman*, *Frederick Douglass*, and *The Wife of His Youth*.

Along with the title story, *Wife* presented "The Sheriff's Children" and seven other tales, including "Uncle Wellington's Wives" and "Her Virginia Mammy." In "Uncle Wellington's Wives," Chesnutt deals with one of his favorite themes, the futility and danger of "color envy." Wellington, a light-skinned, middle-aged former slave who has long been tempted by tales of the good life in the North, leaves his black wife, Milly, and heads for Ohio. There, he gets a good job and marries an Irishwoman. Before long, however, he takes to drink and loses both his job and his white wife.

Chesnutt makes his own views perfectly clear when he creates a black lawyer who tells Wellington that such bad luck was "what you might have expected when you turned your back on your own people and married a white woman. You weren't content with being a slave to the white folks once, but you must try it again. Some people never know when they've got enough." Realizing he has made

Born into slavery in 1817, Frederick Douglass escaped in 1838, then rose to national prominence as a writer, editor, and abolitionist. Chesnutt, who had long admired the fiery black leader, wrote a young readers' biography of him in 1899.

some bad mistakes, Wellington returns to the forgiving Milly, a hardworking, independent woman with few illusions and no pretensions.

"Her Virginia Mammy," another color-line story, presents Clara Hohlfelder, the beautiful stepdaughter of a German family in Groveland, Ohio. Clara, who knows nothing of her ancestry—as a baby, she was rescued from the Mississippi River after a steamboat explosion—is adored by the aristocratic New Englander, John Winthrop. She returns his love, but hesitates to marry him because of her lack of known background.

When the black "Mrs. Harper"—in reality, Clara's birth mother—finds her child after years of searching, she decides to identify herself only as the girl's onetime "mammy," or nursemaid. Clara, she tells her daughter, is the offspring of two distinguished white Virginia families. Now persuaded that she can add luster to John's family tree, Clara agrees to marry him as Mrs. Harper looks on with mixed heartbreak and joy.

The Conjure Woman and *The Wife of His Youth and Other Stories of the Color Line* garnered a number of glowing reviews. "The two volumes taken together constitute an important addition, not only to our literature, but to our knowledge of the negro race," said a critic for *Outlook* magazine. Singling out "The Wife of His Youth," he called it one of "the best short stories in American literature."

An article in *Town Topics* asserted that Chesnutt was "pre-eminently qualified to bring the resources of his exclusive domain into effective and artistic presentation"—in other words, Chesnutt was writing about a subject he knew better than anyone else, and he was a good enough writer to produce great stories about it. William Dean Howells called Chesnutt's stories "new and fresh and strong," and said they had "won the ear of the more intelligent public."

James Lane Allen, author of such best-selling romantic works as *Flute and Violin* and *The Kentucky Cardinal*, joined the chorus of admirers. Writing about Chesnutt's new books to his friend Walter Page (who passed the letter on to a highly pleased Chesnutt), Allen said, "I went through ['The Wife of His Youth'] without drawing breath—except to laugh out two or three times. It is the freshest, firmest, most admirably held in & wrought out little story that has gladdened—and moistened—my eyes in many months."

But because all the stories in *The Wife of His Youth* deal with the effects of race mixing—a subject guaranteed to unsettle many Americans of the era—some readers found the book shocking, even repulsive. A white reviewer for one important conservative publication, the *Bookman*, did offer patronizing praise for the title story, which involves no direct contact between blacks and whites. The critic called this story "a subtle psychological study of the negro's spiritual nature," which revealed "secret depths of the dusky soul."

But the rest of *The Wife of His Youth* was "hardly worthy of mention," sneered the *Bookman*'s reviewer. "A graver fault than its lack of literary quality is its careless approach to the all but unapproachable ground of sentimental relations between the black race and the white race." In short, wailed the *Bookman*, Chesnutt showed "a lamentable lack of tact" and "a reckless disregard of matters respected by more experienced writers." In this commentator's view, blacks and whites could be shown as master and servant, but the suggestion of any other attachment bordered on the criminal.

Despite such detractors, *The Wife of His Youth* and *The Conjure Woman* firmly established Chesnutt's literary reputation, confirming him as the era's most important black fiction writer. ✦

Dazzled by "The Wife of His Youth," popular white author James Lane Allen (above) wrote to Walter Page: "Who—in the name of the Lord!" he asked, "is Charles W. Chesnutt?" Although Kentucky novelist Allen specialized in "plantation fiction" himself, he came to be one of Chesnutt's most enthusiastic fans.

6

RENA, AT LAST!

Attorney-stenographer Chesnutt writes a legal brief with one hand; with the other, author Chesnutt writes short stories and novels (including the one he perches on, The House Behind the Cedars). Cleveland's principal newspaper, the Plain Dealer, ran this admiring caricature in 1904.

CHARLES CHESNUTT HAD always wanted to write full-time, but his literary efforts had never produced enough money to support his family, particularly after his daughters entered college. By the fall of 1899, however, the sales prospects of *The Conjure Woman*, *The Wife of His Youth*, and *Frederick Douglass* looked extremely promising, and Chesnutt decided to take the plunge. With his wife in full agreement, he closed his court-reporting business and settled down to his writing table.

At this point, the author had two novels in progress: one, "Rena Walden," had been on his mind for more than a decade. Rena, whom Chesnutt biographer Frances Richardson Keller (*An American Crusade*) calls "Chesnutt's literary love," had first appeared in an unpublished color-line short story. She later turned into a novelette (short novel), then back into a short story, then into a full-fledged novel.

Because Chesnutt often destroyed work that displeased him, the total number of "Rena" manuscripts is unknown, but 5, varying in length from 39 to 231 manuscript pages, survive. Clearly, Rena Walden obsessed her creator: If he did nothing else, Chesnutt vowed, he would put her into a book. As he put it in a letter to Walter Page, "I have not slept with that story for ten years without falling in love with it and believing in it."

65

Smith College's class of 1901—which included Ethel and Helen Chesnutt (circled)—gathers for a portrait in 1899. Although Charles Chesnutt was responsible for paying for his older daughters' education as well as that of his two younger children, Edwin and Dorothy, he nevertheless quit his profitable court stenography business and took up full-time writing.

Although his heart was with Rena, Chesnutt had higher hopes for the publication of "The Rainbow Chasers," a more conventional novel, and one unlikely to offend anyone. If he could capture a large, "genteel" audience with this book, Chesnutt reasoned, he could then publish the kind of "problem" novel he really wanted to write.

"The Rainbow Chasers" tells the rather well-worn story of a shy, middle-aged bachelor who agrees to help a younger man win the hand of a beautiful young widow. After she inherits a surprise fortune, the widow makes it clear that she has loved the older man—who has meanwhile proven himself a hero—all along. The two marry, demonstrating that happiness often lies close at hand rather than at the end of a rainbow.

The editors at Houghton Mifflin, who had turned down "Rena Walden" more than once, greeted "The

RENA, AT LAST! 67

Rainbow Chasers" with limited enthusiasm. "There is a certain unreality about these [characters]," said Walter Page, "that prevents them from being interesting." Nevertheless, the Boston editors decided the novel possessed "homely sincerity" and "freedom from affectation," and agreed to publish it.

At about this time, Walter Page left Houghton Mifflin to go into business with another publisher. He also changed his mind about "Rena Walden": In January 1900, he wrote Chesnutt and said the new firm of Doubleday, Page would like to publish it. Delighted, Chesnutt hastened to board an eastbound train. When he met with Page, the editor suggested a name change for the novel—from "Rena Walden" to *The House Behind the Cedars*.

Chesnutt next called on Houghton Mifflin. News in the literary world travels fast; the Boston editors had already heard that their former colleague, Page, wanted "Rena." Although they had rejected it several times, Page's interest kindled their own, and they now asked for "the privilege of reconsidering [it]." Within a few weeks, they sent Chesnutt a letter: "We have decided to take "Rena" (under the title *The House Behind the Cedars*) in place of *The Rainbow Chasers*, and to publish it next fall."

Elated but worried about Page, Chesnutt asked his old friend what to do. Page told Chesnutt to go with Houghton Mifflin, which had already published two of his books; besides, he said, its imprint would add to the book's prestige. If the Boston group changed its mind, Page added, he would be more than willing to publish the book. Grateful for the editor's honesty, Chesnutt signed a contract with Houghton Mifflin, which published *The House Behind the Cedars* in 1900.

Most of his work, Chesnutt once explained, "dealt with the problems of people of mixed blood, which, while [largely] the same as the true Negro, are in some

. . . respects much more complex and difficult." It is these "problems" that form the heart of *The House Behind the Cedars*, generally considered Chesnutt's finest novel—as well as his most autobiographical work. "There is scarcely an incident in it," said its author, "that has not been paralleled in real life to my actual knowledge."

The House Behind the Cedars tells the story of Rena and John Walden, a very light-skinned mulatto sister and brother born in fictional Patesville, North Carolina, soon after the Civil War. As soon as he can, John moves to Clarence, South Carolina, where he changes his name, becomes a wealthy lawyer, buys a plantation, and lives as a white man. In Chesnutt's view, "passing" made a certain amount of sense: Although it put a mulatto in a "false position," he said, passing also enabled him or her to "enjoy the rights and dignities of citizenship," which a segregated society reserved for whites.

John Walden believes that, as a human being, he is "entitled to a chance in life," and that if his "whiteness" can provide that chance, he would be a fool not to use it. Asserting that Rena, his beautiful, equally fair-skinned sister, also deserves that chance, John brings her to South Carolina, where she becomes engaged to a white aristocrat named George Tryon. Chesnutt explains Rena's agreement to follow her brother across the color line: "To be white had been so long synonymous with wealth and position . . . that she bowed to the symbol [of a white skin] without any special thought of what it signified."

George, however, discovers Rena's racial origins and breaks their engagement. Ignoring her brother's pleas, Rena returns to Patesville. "I shall never marry any man," she says. "God is against it; I'll stay with my own people." In Patesville, Jeff Wain, an apparently upstanding mulatto citizen, offers Rena a job as

THE HOUSE BEHIND THE CEDARS,

9 Pt.

Time touches all things with destroying hand; and if he seem now and then to bestow the bloom of youth, the sap of Spring, it is but a brief mockery, to be surely and swiftly followed by the wrinkles of old age, the dry leaves and bare branches of Winter.   And yet there are places where Time seems to linger lovingly, long after youth has departed, and to which he seems loath to bring the evil day.   Who has not known some even-tempered old man or woman, who seemed to have drunk of the fountain of youth?   Who has not seen somewhere an old town, that, having long since ceased to grow, yet held its own without perceptible decline?

Some such trite reflection -- as apposite to the subject as most random reflections are -- passed through the mind of a young man who came out of the front door of the Patesville Hotel about nine o'clock one fine morning in Spring, a few years after the Civil

This manuscript page, which Chesnutt typed and corrected in 1899, is part of at least the fifth version of his much-reworked story of Rena Walden. "If labor endears a particular piece to an author," observed one literary critic, "then The House Behind the Cedars should have been Chesnutt's favorite."

a country schoolteacher. She accepts and moves to distant Sampson County—which happens to be George Tryon's home ground.

Glimpsing Rena outside the schoolhouse, George realizes he loves only her: "His stubborn heart simply would not let go," observes the narrator. George now sees that "custom was tyranny," and that "love was the only law," and he asks Rena to come back to him. On the same day, she receives unwelcome but insistent advances from Wain.

Distraught, Rena once again takes off for Patesville, which lies beyond the treacherous cypress swamps along the Cape Fear River. She collapses on the way and is found by Frank Fowler, a faithful black childhood friend who carries her home; there, she dies. Frank, she thinks in her last moments, loved her "best of them all."

Chesnutt makes his views of the Waldens' passing clear. "Let him uncurl his scornful lip and come down from the pedestal of superiority, to which assured position and wide opportunity have lifted him," the book's narrator says, "and put himself in the place of

Author William Dean Howells, late-19th-century America's foremost literary figure, recognized Chesnutt as a major talent. Calling Chesnutt's stories "new and fresh and strong as life itself," Howells said they should be valued both for their "very great racial interest" and "simply as works of art."

Rena and her brother, upon whom God had lavished his best gifts, and from whom society would have withheld all that made these gifts valuable. To undertake what they tried to do required great courage."

Chesnutt knew that *The House Behind the Cedars* would get heavy criticism in the South. "Any discussion of the race problem from any but the ultra Southern point of view naturally would," he told his publisher. Yet he hoped for a positive response in the rest of the country. In terms of literary criticism, he got it.

Southern publications predictably hated the book: The Alabama magazine the *Bookworm*, for example, disgustedly noted that Chesnutt obviously favored "race equality." But northern critics, both black and white, applauded. "What Chesnutt feels and makes his readers feel," said the Boston *Budget's* reviewer, "is that Negroes must be treated always as human beings." Other critics called the work "thought-provoking" and an "interesting 'problem novel.'"

Literature fans have continued to find the novel absorbing. "To several generations of Afro-American readers," notes William Andrews (in his 1980 book, *The Literary Career of Charles W. Chesnutt*) *"The House Behind the Cedars* ranked as black fiction's signal achievement, rivaled only, perhaps, by James Weldon Johnson's *The Autobiography of an Ex-Coloured Man* (1912)." Darwin Turner, who wrote the introduction for the 1976 edition of *House*, comments, "In the development of Negro literature in America, *The House Behind the Cedars* holds a place of great social and historical importance. It demands to be read."

Chesnutt, as Howells had asserted, may have "won the ear of the more intelligent public," but in 1900, surprisingly few white readers sought out books by black authors; even fewer, apparently, wanted to read books that took a realistic attitude toward the nation's race problems. The novel's modest sales figures—some 3,000 Americans bought the book—were somewhat disappointing, but neither author nor publisher was discouraged.

In fact, the words of praise that the book received prompted not only Houghton Mifflin but another publishing house, Harper and Brothers, to ask Chesnutt for a new novel at once. Representing Harper's, the eminent William Dean Howells wrote to Chesnutt and requested a manuscript "about the color-line, and of as actual and immediate interest as possible." Immensely flattered by Howells's invitation, Chesnutt nevertheless stayed with his original publisher. His next book, he assured his daughters in an October 1900 letter, was bound to be "a howling success."

The author based his second—and most ambitious—novel, *The Marrow of Tradition*, on a real historical event: an 1898 racial attack that had left more than 20 blacks dead in Wilmington, North Carolina, a city 85 miles from Fayetteville. Chesnutt saw the bloody incident as "an outbreak of pure, malignant and altogether indefensible race prejudice," but to make sure he was right, he paid a visit to the South—his first in 17 years. His long absence, he thought, had put him somewhat out of touch, particularly with the so-called New South and its rush toward invincible white supremacy.

Chesnutt's 1901 trip took him to Wilmington, Fayetteville, and other southern communities where he interviewed black and white citizens and visited schools, factories, and town halls. After about a month, he returned to Cleveland and started what would turn out to be an eight-month writing marathon. He had high hopes that *The Marrow of Tradition*, as he confided to his publisher, could "become lodged in the popular mind as the legitimate success-

Reporting on the racial violence that rocked Wilmington, North Carolina, in 1898, Collier's Weekly magazine showed armed blacks on a murderous rampage. In truth, however, the conflict—which inspired Chesnutt's 1901 novel about racism, The Marrow of Tradition—involved the slaughter of unarmed blacks by rioting white supremacists.

135,000 SETS, 270,000 VOLUMES SOLD.

UNCLE TOM'S CABIN

FOR SALE HERE.

AN EDITION FOR THE MILLION, COMPLETE IN 1 Vol., PRICE 37 1-2 CENTS.
"   "   IN GERMAN, IN 1 Vol., PRICE 50 CENTS.
"   "   IN 2 Vols,. CLOTH, 6 PLATES, PRICE $1.50.
SUPERB ILLUSTRATED EDITION, IN 1 Vol., WITH 153 ENGRAVINGS,
PRICES FROM $2.50 TO $5.00.

The Greatest Book of the Age.

An 1852 advertisement promotes Harriet Beecher Stowe's Uncle Tom's Cabin, *the phenomenally popular novel that provoked a wave of opposition to slavery and helped start the Civil War. Chesnutt hoped* The Marrow of Tradition *would become the "legitimate successor" to Stowe's influential best-seller, but the public greeted the new book coldly.*

or of *Uncle Tom's Cabin* [Harriet Beecher Stowe's 1852 blockbuster best-seller about slavery] as depicting an epoch in our national history."

Chesnutt put everything he had into *The Marrow of Tradition*. The novel includes plots and subplots concerning not only southern politics and the Ku Klux Klan but racial prejudice, romance, family loyalty, murder, revenge, justice, and forgiveness. Central to the action are two families: the white, socially prominent Carterets and the mulatto Millers. Olivia Carteret and Janet Miller are daughters of the same white father, but Olivia's mother was white; Janet's, black.

Hoping to end a local trend toward black political equality, Major Philip Carteret (Olivia's husband) conspires with two other white racists to get rid of the town's elected black officials. The planned coup triggers a race riot that kills a number of blacks, including the son of Janet Miller and her husband, Dr. Adam Miller.

Soon after the riot, the Carterets realize that their only child, Felix, is dying. Only one man can save him: Dr. Adam Miller. Blaming Carteret for both his son's death and the burning of his hospital, Miller refuses to operate on Felix.

Olivia has treated her half sister badly, cheating her of a share in their father's estate and even refusing to speak to her in public. Now bitterly repenting her cruelty, she begs Janet to persuade Adam to save Felix. Janet searches her heart and discovers that family ties, forgiveness, and love outweigh race, revenge, and hatred; she does as Olivia asks. At first unmoved by his wife's impassioned plea for Felix's life, Adam finally decides she is right; repaying murder with mercy, he saves the boy.

The Marrow of Tradition enraged the South. At some points, in fact, the book seems deliberately intended to offend conservative whites. For example, as Dr. Miller gazes at his fire-gutted hospital and thinks despairingly of the riot's black dead, he decides that there is one sure "guaranty of the future": the knowledge that even under the worst conditions, blacks have survived and even flourished:

> The negro was here before the Anglo-Saxon was evolved, and his thick lips and heavy-lidded eyes looked out from the inscrutable face of the Sphinx across the sands of Egypt while . . . the ancestors of those who now oppress him were living in caves, practicing human sacrifice, and painting themselves with woad [blue dye]—and the negro is here yet.

Expecting to sell at least 20,000 copies, Houghton Mifflin published *The Marrow of Tradition* in Octo-

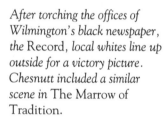

After torching the offices of Wilmington's black newspaper, the Record, *local whites line up outside for a victory picture. Chesnutt included a similar scene in* The Marrow of Tradition.

ber 1901. It ignited a literary fire storm. Southern reviewers, of course, trashed the book. Surprisingly, most praised Chesnutt's writing, which they called "strong," "vigorous," and "earnest," but they could not forgive him for, as a Kansas City critic put it, "arguing for the equality of the colored race, political and social equality." One southern reviewer called the novel "an insidious book" because the author's cure for the race problem "would seem to be intermarriage of the races." Others damned it for being "angry," "vindictive," "unnatural," and "fanatical."

Northerners were more positive, calling the book "honest" and "realistic," "powerful but painful." The critic for the *New Bedford Morning Mercury* in Massachusetts wrote: "Those who are willing face a great question, and to see the bearings of that question as they really are, will find in *The Marrow of Tradition*

a recital not merely to stir to the blood, but to enlighten the mind and awaken the conscience."

In an era when popular-novel readers demanded star-crossed lovers and happy endings, when they liked tales set in picture-perfect American towns, when they thrilled to the drumbeats of progress and national unity, a book like *The Marrow of Tradition* was doomed from the start. Even one of Chesnutt's close friends, Chicago state's attorney Charles Deneen, qualified his praise for the book. "The subject of your excellent work," he told Chesnutt, "is not one that will commend it to the general public. The truths you portray are unwelcome ones."

William Dean Howells also worried about *Marrow*'s "bitterness of tone," but he remained one of Chesnutt's warmest admirers. "No one who reads the book," he said, "can deny that the case is pre-

Helen Maria (top) and Ethel Perry Chesnutt (bottom) sat for these portraits in 1901, the year they graduated from Smith College. Ethel would later marry and raise a family; Helen, who remained single, would write a 1952 biography of her father, Charles Waddell Chesnutt, Pioneer of the Color Line.

sented with great power, or fail to recognize in the writer a portent of the sort of negro equality against which no series of hangings and burnings will finally avail."

Two months after its appearance, *The Marrow of Tradition* had sold 5,000 copies, a respectable number but not enough to justify the unusually high sums Houghton Mifflin had spent on advertising and promotion. Chesnutt now faced an unhappy fact: "I am beginning to suspect that the public as a rule does not care for books in which the principal characters are colored people," he told the publisher.

Chesnutt's friends, he added, had been trying to persuade him to write about people other than blacks. "They suggest further," he reported sadly, "that considering the extent to which I have been advertised as a member of that race, I might do [the race] just as much good by a worthy achievement in some other field, as by writing books about them which the public does not care for. I am beginning [to feel] somewhat the same way."

"A man must live and consider his family," Chesnutt told his daughter Ethel after *The Marrow of Tradition*'s publication in October 1901. Ethel and Helen had graduated from Smith in May, but Edwin was then studying for the Harvard College entrance exam, and fifth-grader Dorothy would be ready for college in a few years. In early 1902, Chesnutt closed his writer's notebook and reopened his court-reporting business, marking the second time he had put his family's needs ahead of his writing career. He had little trouble restarting his old operation, and was soon as busy with it as ever.

Harvard accepted Edwin, who entered the college in the fall of 1902. Ethel accepted a teaching job at Tuskegee, but soon returned to Cleveland to marry Edwin Williams, a librarian at Case Western Reserve University. When the couple had a son, Charles

The Chesnutt family moved into this dwelling on Cleveland's affluent, tree-lined Lamont Avenue in 1904. Charles, who resided in the comfortable 14-room house for the rest of his life, spent most of his free time reading and writing in his book-lined study.

Waddell Chesnutt Williams, they moved in with Ethel's parents. Helen, too, returned to live with the family and quickly landed a job teaching Latin at Cleveland's Central High School.

Helen Chesnutt was popular with her pupils; one of them later called her "a whale of a good Latin teacher," and another said she was "a dedicated teacher who loved her students and who exerted a lot of influence over them." Among Helen's warmest admirers—and later, closest friends—was 13-year-old Langston Hughes, a budding poet whose first works appeared in the Central High School literary magazine.

The extended Chesnutt family needed more room, and in May 1904, they moved to an elegant house on Cleveland's Lamont Avenue. A friend described the place as "an affluent house of the 1890s, not shrieking with innovations, but furnished with good antique furniture." The Chesnutts' new home, said another observer, was "beautiful," with "a wide porch and 40 windows and polished hardwood floors in the spacious rooms. An entrance hall was large enough to serve as a dance floor and to accommodate an orchestra at Christmas parties. There was a library for Charles." In this house, Charles Chesnutt would live for the rest of his life. ☙

7

PEN AGAINST PREJUDICE

America's most influential black man, educator Booker T. Washington, urged blacks to put economic independence ahead of social and political equality. America's leading black author, Charles Chesnutt, disagreed vehemently—he called Washington's approach "short-sighted, expensive, troublesome, and ridiculous"—but the two nonetheless maintained a close friendship.

WHEREAS CHARLES CHESNUTT was the most prominent black fiction writer of his time, the best-known black American in any arena was Booker T. Washington. Born into slavery in 1856, Washington remained a slave until the Civil War ended, then worked in the salt furnaces and coal mines of West Virginia. At age 16, he enrolled at Hampton Institute, an industrial school for blacks; upon graduating, he became a teacher; and in 1881, he founded a school that he patterned after Hampton: Tuskegee Normal and Industrial Institute, in Tuskegee, Alabama. By the end of the 19th century, it was America's largest and best-endowed black institution.

All the while, Washington worked tirelessly to uplift his race. His success at Tuskegee and his widely read autobiography, *Up from Slavery*, which related how he had built the school brick by brick, helped publicize his efforts. But it was his widely hailed "solution" to America's race problem that established him as the country's leading black spokesman.

The key moment in Washington's rise to national prominence took place at Atlanta's Cotton States

Female students attend a Tuskegee Institute sewing class in 1902. Founded by Booker T. Washington in 1881, the institute stressed courses in practical money-making skills rather than academic subjects such as philosophy or literature. Most whites agreed with Washington's priorities, but many idealistic blacks—including Chesnutt—considered them misplaced.

and International Exposition in 1895, when he delivered the landmark speech now known as the Atlanta Compromise. Washington exhorted blacks to delay their campaign for political, social, and intellectual equality and concentrate on improving themselves through practical education, industriousness, and racial solidarity. "The wisest among my race understand," he said, "that the agitation of questions of social equality is the extremest folly." Blacks, he believed, would be granted social and political equality only after they had won their economic independence from whites.

Washington's racial program won the enthusiastic support of white America. He was not without his critics, however, and most of them were black. Among those who disagreed vigorously with the Tuskegee principal was Charles Chesnutt.

Chesnutt first met Washington in 1901, during a trip south to research material for *The Marrow of Tradition.* The two men quickly became friends; they became so well acquainted, in fact, that two of Chesnutt's children, Ethel and Edwin, worked for Washington at Tuskegee, and a third, Helen, spent a summer with the Washingtons. Chesnutt and Washington liked and respected one another in spite of their differing views on the race problem. Each man knew that the other was deeply concerned about the fate of black Americans.

Yet this shared interest did not stop Chesnutt from discussing their differences privately or in public. He wrote in the March 31, 1901, issue of the *Cleveland Leader* that Washington's accommodationist approach was "not only short-sighted, expensive and troublesome" but "borders on the ridiculous." Chesnutt added that "the present writer does not believe in the wisdom of the separation of the races which prevails in the Southern States, and thinks that it is carried to an extreme."

One of the points of Washington's program that most troubled Chesnutt concerned the right to vote. Chesnutt was outraged that southern blacks were being robbed of their voting rights through the passage of laws that discriminated against blacks, as well as through lynching and other acts meant to scare them away from the polls. He maintained that blacks could never enjoy the fruits of freedom so long as they lacked their full civil rights.

Over the years, Chesnutt expressed this view to Washington in several letters. "It is very difficult," Washington wrote in one response, "for any law making body to give an individual influence or power which he does not intrinsically possess." He added that every black should demand his constitutional rights but "will have to depend upon the influence which he can bring to bear in his own immediate community for his ultimate defense and final rights." According to Washington, blacks did not possess the political clout to win these rights.

Washington, always a realist, pointed out to Chesnutt that people vote every few years but must eat, work, and send their children to school every day. Chesnutt, however, was not convinced by this line of reasoning. "The importance of a thing," he responded, "is not to be measured by the number of times you do it." Then he cited a few examples to help prove his point: "Birth. Death. Marriage."

Chesnutt put a lot of effort into trying to sway Washington's position on voting rights because the Tuskegee educator was the best connected, most politically powerful black man in the nation. Yet Chesnutt did not limit his campaign against disfranchisement to his discussions and correspondence with Washington. In 1903, James Pott and Company published *The Negro Problem, A Series of Articles by Representative American Negroes Today*. This book contained essays by Washington; the noted scholar

W. E. B. Du Bois works in his office at Atlanta University in 1909. The scholar and activist was also editor of The Crisis, *the official publication of the National Association for the Advancement of Colored People (NAACP). Like Chesnutt, Du Bois disagreed strongly with Washington's position on black civil rights.*

W. E. B. Du Bois; the poet Paul Laurence Dunbar;
and many other of the nation's best-known blacks.
Chesnutt contributed "The Disfranchisement of the
Negro," an essay in which he claimed that "the rights
of the Negroes are at a lower ebb than at any time
during the thirty-five years of their freedom, and the
race prejudice more intense and uncompromising."

"The Disfranchisement of the Negro" describes
how southern legislators prevented blacks from
voting by circumventing the Fifteenth Amendment,
which had guaranteed every man the right to vote.
It was the aim of southern legislators, Chesnutt wrote,
to "violate the spirit of the Federal Constitution by
disfranchising the Negro, while seeming to respect its
letter by avoiding the mention of race or color."
People in some southern states, for example, could
not vote unless they owned $300 worth of personal
property. In Virginia, they had to be able to read and
explain any clause in the Constitution before casting
a ballot. In Alabama, they had to be employed
regularly. (Because such conditions kept many whites
as well as blacks from voting, some southern states
decreed that any descendant of a Civil War veteran
could vote. This new wrinkle gave the vote to
virtually everyone who was white—and to almost no
one who was black.)

"The Disfranchisement of the Negro" made it
clear that voting restrictions affected all blacks, even
those who could vote. Politicians were free to ignore
black interests because they did not have to court
black voters for help in winning an election. "No
judge is rendered careful," Chesnutt observed, "no
sheriff diligent, for fear that he may offend a black
constituency."

Chesnutt called for blacks to fight against disfranchisement by taking legal action and bringing the
issue before the courts. "The Constitution is clear and
unequivocal in its terms," he wrote, "and no Supreme

Honoring its Civil War veterans, a North Carolina town stages a Memorial Day parade in 1909. For decades after the war ended in 1865, some southern states kept blacks from the polls with a devious but simple trick: To cast a ballot, a voter had to be a Confederate veteran or the descendant of one—and therefore, of course, white. Chesnutt lashed out at such practices in his widely read 1903 essay "The Disfranchisement of the Negro."

Court can indefinitely continue to construe it as meaning anything but what it says. This Court should be bombarded with suits until it makes some definite pronouncement, one way or the other." Chesnutt ended the article by saying that blacks could and should appeal to God for justice, for they were on the side of right.

Among Chesnutt's published works, "The Disfranchisement of the Negro" was followed by a story in a somewhat lighter vein. In June 1904, the *Atlantic* published "Baxter's Procrustes," his seventh story to appear in the magazine. Widely regarded as the best piece of short fiction he ever wrote, the tale mocks an organization of literary collectors who are more interested in the commercial value of a book than in its contents. The story is loosely based on an incident that took place in 1902, when Cleveland's prestigious Rowfant Club denied Chesnutt membership, apparently because it was not yet ready to open its doors to blacks.

Just as "Baxter's Procrustes" was being prepared for publication, Houghton Mifflin informed Chesnutt that it had decided not to accept a novel he was working on, *The Colonel's Dream*, because "the public has failed to respond adequately to your other admirable work in this line." He promptly turned to Walter Page, who had helped him with *The House Behind the Cedars*. Page had formed his own publishing house with Frank Doubleday, and their company published Chesnutt's third—and, as it turned out, last—novel the following year, in 1905.

The Colonel's Dream marked one of Chesnutt's last efforts to address racial matters through a work of fiction. "I have almost decided to foreswear the race problem stories," he had told Page in 1904, "but I should like to write a good one which would be widely read, before I quit." He hoped *The Colonel's Dream* was that book.

Members of Cleveland's exclusive Rowfant Club assemble for a meeting in the early 1900s. Chesnutt, perhaps taking subtle revenge on the club for its refusal to admit him in 1902, satirized it in his highly praised 1904 short story, "Baxter's Procrustes." Finally reversing its admissions policy, the Rowfant Club made Chesnutt its first black member in 1910.

Charles and Edwin Chesnutt enjoy a sunny afternoon together in 1918. Highly organized himself, Charles had often fretted about his son, whom he considered indecisive. After graduating from Harvard, Edwin traveled abroad, decided to work for an oil company in Cuba, became a stenographer, then spent a year teaching at Tuskegee. At last, to his father's relief, he earned a dental degree from Northwestern University and settled down to a successful career as a dentist.

Colonel Henry French, the novel's white protagonist, is a successful northern businessman who moves back to the southern town of his birth. He quickly realizes that Clarendon, North Carolina, has changed from his boyhood days. The town, like much of the South, is in the midst of an economic depression and has become quite run-down. Daily life in Clarendon has been made even worse by the evil Bill Fetters, who controls the town because he owns its chief industry, a cotton mill. Fetters pays the townspeople slaves' wages to work at his mill. He also practices a form of slavery by auctioning off local convicts as laborers.

Eager to bring the town into "contact with the outer world and its more advanced thought," French decides to build his own cotton mill. His ambition is to turn Clarendon into "a busy hive of industry, where no man, and no woman obliged to work, need be without employment at fair wages; where the trinity of peace, prosperity and progress would reign supreme, where men like Fetters and methods like his would no longer be tolerated." The colonel also seeks to destroy the convict labor auction and wishes to improve the quality of education for blacks and whites.

At first, French believes that bringing about change will be a simple matter. But he soon meets with resistance, and by the end of the novel Fetters has succeeded in thwarting his efforts at every turn. The mill is only half-completed; the schools remain unimproved; the townspeople are no more enlightened than they were before the colonel arrived. His dream of progress shattered, French concludes that Clarendon will never change, and he returns to the North, defeated.

Chesnutt's message—that the New South is stuck in the present, with no plans for its future—came through loud and clear. Many reviewers felt, however, that the narrative preached far too much. *The Colonel's Dream* received a great deal of attention and a fair share of favorable reviews, both in the United States and abroad. But even those critics who praised the novel cited it as being deliberate and full of editorializing, and the work soon lapsed into obscurity.

In June 1905, around the time that *The Colonel's Dream* was being published, Chesnutt traveled to Boston to attend his son's graduation from Harvard College. During his visit, the senior Chesnutt gave a speech entitled "Race Prejudice: Its Causes and Its Cure" at the Boston Literary and Historical Association.

After outlining the origins of racial prejudice in America, Chesnutt said that "the sole policy of race separation is illogical and unjust and must sooner or later fall by its own weight. . . . I not only believe that the admixture of the races will in time become an accomplished fact, but I believe that it will be a good thing for all concerned."

Then, offering a sentiment that would be echoed more than half a century later by Martin Luther King, Jr., Chesnutt told the audience, "I see an epoch in our nation's history, not in my time nor in yours, but in the not too distant future . . . when men will be esteemed and honored for their character and their talents."

Chesnutt outraged a number of people with his mention of the two races mixing, and he received a flood of angry, abusive letters and hurtful press coverage. Nevertheless, this speech, along with his fiction and his essays, established him as a thoughtful advocate for black rights. Accordingly, he was invited in 1905 to fill an opening in the Committee of Twelve for the Advancement of the Interests of the Negro Race, a powerful group whose stated aim was "to turn the attention of the race to the importance of constructive, progressive effort, and the attention of the country to Negro successes." Booker T. Washington, *New York Age* editor T. Thomas Fortune, and educator Kelly Miller were among the committee's 12 original members.

There was plenty of work for the committee to do. In August 1906, black soldiers stationed at Fort Brown in Brownsville, Texas, were blamed by the town's white citizens for starting a riot; after looking hastily into the matter, President Theodore Roosevelt instructed Secretary of War William Howard Taft to dishonorably discharge 167 men of the 25th Infantry Regiment. One month later, another major race riot occurred, this time in Atlanta, Georgia. (It was similar in many ways to

the outbreak of violence that Chesnutt had written about in *The Marrow of Tradition*.)

Just as upsetting to Chesnutt was a decision handed down by the U.S. Supreme Court in 1908. Four years earlier, the Kentucky legislature had ruled that blacks and whites could not be educated at the same school, as was true of Berea College. When the Supreme Court upheld the decision and banned integrated education in Kentucky, Chesnutt wrote to Booker T. Washington that the ruling set a precedent, for "what one state may do, another state may do."

When another race riot broke out in 1908, this time in Springfield, Illinois, the hometown of

Ku Klux Klan riders pursue black Union troops in The Birth of a Nation, *a controversial but hugely successful 1915 film that depicts blacks as violent rapists and Klan members as avenging heroes. Insisting that the movie aimed only at "stirring up race prejudice and race hatred," Chesnutt campaigned—successfully—against its appearance in Cleveland.*

Abraham Lincoln, the consequences were dramatic. A journalist named William English Walling witnessed the violence and wrote a powerful article in which he issued a plea "to treat the Negro on a plane of absolute political and social equality." Several prominent northerners were deeply moved by what Walling wrote, and they agreed to organize a national race conference to be held in New York City at the end of May.

Chesnutt was among the 60 people to attend the conference, as were W. E. B. Du Bois and William Monroe Trotter, publisher of the *Boston Guardian*, an influential black newspaper. (Booker T. Washington was also invited to the proceedings but chose not to attend.) The atmosphere throughout the three-day session was unusually tense because many of the black leaders were suspicious of their white colleagues, who had called for the meeting.

Ultimately, however, the gathering was a success. The group formed a permanent organization, the National Negro Committee (NNC), to carry on its work. Several more conferences were held during the next few months, and in May 1910 the NNC held its second annual meeting, at which time the organization that Chesnutt had a hand in founding received a new name: the National Association for the Advancement of Colored People (NAACP).

One month later, Chesnutt was working in his office when he collapsed suddenly. His employees rushed him to Huron Road Hospital, where he remained unconscious for several days. According to his doctor, Chesnutt had suffered a stroke and had to remain bedridden. His family rallied around him, and by mid-July he was strong enough to leave his bed. His physician advised him not to exert himself.

Chesnutt slipped back into his old ways, however, and before long he was as busy as ever. He took care of his business obligations and continued to put his influence to good use, becoming especially active in the NAACP's Cleveland branch. As the decade wore on, membership in various organizations also took up much of his time.

In 1910, Chesnutt became the first black member of the Rowfant Club, which had denied him admission eight years earlier. Extremely proud of this honor, he wrote a number of essays—including "Who and Why Was Samuel Johnson," "The Life and Works of Alexandre Dumas," and "Francois Villon, Man and Poet"—that he read at club meetings. In 1911, he became president of the Cleveland Council of Sociology, which he had joined in 1905. And in 1912, he was elected to the board of directors of the Cleveland Chamber of Commerce, an organization of businessmen and professionals.

All the while, Chesnutt wrote works of fiction in his spare time, but no one would agree to publish them, partly because his books had never been very profitable and partly because dialect fiction had become outdated. Undeterred, he continued to write, filing away story after story when it became clear they would not be published. He refused to put his pen aside even after Small, Maynard and Company, which had issued his young reader's biography of Frederick Douglass in 1899, rejected "Aunt Hagar's Children," a collection of stories, in 1919.

Chesnutt was no stranger to laboring in obscurity; he had done it many times before. But he had no way of knowing that after *The Colonel's Dream*, he would never publish another major work. Still, in the years that followed, his voice would continue to be heard. ❧

8

A CASTLE IN THE AIR

❧

THE 1920s BROUGHT America the Jazz Age: Flappers cropped their hair, raised their hemlines, and smoked Sweet Caporals; their boyfriends wore raccoon coats, drove snappy roadsters, and drank bathtub gin; everybody danced the Charleston. But the decade produced more than such froth; beneath the giddy bubbles, a powerful tide was rising.

The Roaring Twenties introduced the Harlem Renaissance, an unprecedented outpouring of black art, literature, and music. Suddenly dazzling the nation was an explosion of new talent—a galaxy of black artists that included poets Langston Hughes, Countee Cullen, and Claude McKay; writers Walter White, Zora Neale Hurston, Jean Toomer, James Weldon Johnson, and Alain Locke; musicians Louis Armstrong, Eubie Blake, and Duke Ellington; artists Archibald Motley and Aaron Douglas.

Dominating this artistic revolution was a symbolic figure whom Locke named "the New Negro." Radical on race matters, the New Negro did "not fear the face of day"; he was "breaking his shell and beginning to bask in the sunlight of real manhood."

Visiting California in 1915, Chesnutt (second from left), his wife (center), and friends drive through a giant sequoia tree. Chesnutt bought his first car in 1914, the year in which increasing automobile use forced Ohio to set speed limits: 8 miles per hour downtown, 15 in the suburbs.

Flappers take part in a nightclub Charleston contest in 1926. The century's third decade—the Roaring Twenties—featured flappers, bathtub gin, and jazz; the era also introduced the Harlem Renaissance, an explosion of black American art, literature, and music. Chesnutt tried to keep up with the times, but his fiction was rooted in another age, and editors found his later work hopelessly dated.

The New Negro was intellectual, creative, proud of his or her race, and eager to mine the riches of the black heritage. The New Negro was also irreverent, outspoken, and ready to depict the world at its grimmest and most shocking.

Chesnutt, 62 years old at the dawn of the Roaring Twenties and the Harlem Renaissance, was now the acknowledged dean of black American letters. In person and philosophy, he had changed little in a changing world. Rowena Jelliffe, a young woman who met him in Cleveland at about this time, offered this recollection in 1972:

> [Chesnutt] looked like a ruddy Englishman. He had a shock of white hair. He was about 5 feet 9 inches tall and weighed perhaps 155 pounds—not heavy-set at all. He was fair-skinned and he had very striking blue eyes. He was tastefully dressed. He was not foppish or over-fastidious, but he always dressed carefully. He gave the impression of a gentle, inquiring turn of mind. . . . Chesnutt took pride in his black ancestry. His respect for every effort coming out of the black world and for every reaching for equality showed this.

As the Harlem Renaissance rolled into high gear, Chesnutt tried to maintain that respect. "The colored writer of fiction should study life in all its aspects," he said. "Colored novelists," he added, should feel free to write about "Negro characters in the under-world, so long as they do it well." But as the young Renaissance writers expanded on that freedom, producing increasingly raw, gritty, and—to many members of Chesnutt's generation—scandalous work, he grew critical.

"The highest privilege of art," he said in 1926, is "to depict the ideal." His suggestions for appropriate fiction plots included "a Negro oil millionaire, and the difficulty he or she has in keeping his or her money," the adventures of a brave Pullman porter who moonlights as a detective, and a "Negro vision-ary who would . . . bridge the gap between races in a decade." The Renaissance, meanwhile, was awash with poems, novels, and short stories from the ghetto; black writers no longer minced words or flinched from such subjects as murder, rape, incest, and drug use.

This "new realism," Chesnutt felt, had gone too far. Why, he asked, was there "no outstanding noble male character in any of the Negro novels?" Why no females with "heroic attributes"? And why did these young writers concentrate on the "social sub-sewers" and "hectic nightlife" of Harlem?

A writer of sensibility, Chesnutt suggested, might instead choose to portray "the better colored people of New York—not the blatant pleasure-seeking jazz hounds who wasted their substance in dissipation and riotous living, but the self-respecting business and professional men, writers, artists, musicians, actors, teachers and editors, who constituted the worthwhile people of Harlem."

Chesnutt detested much of the Renaissance writers' output, but as a writer himself, he applaud-

Chesnutt strikes a classic tourist pose atop Pikes Peak, Colorado, in 1921. By then financially independent, he began to leave his business operations to a partner and travel extensively; he took his family on long European jaunts and, with his wife, made lengthy explorations of the American West.

ed the sudden willingness of white publishers to take on the work of black authors. Walter White—the remarkable man who wrote best-selling novels, spearheaded the drive against lynching, presided over the NAACP, and served as patron to the young black writers of the 1920s—had long admired both Chesnutt and his fiction. In 1926, White wrote him a letter, urging him to give the world another book.

Chesnutt had not published a novel since *The Colonel's Dream* in 1905, but he respected White, and responded to his suggestion with enthusiasm: "What you say about the reception which a new book by me would receive," he told White, "encourages me to see what I can do."

Chesnutt now had the time to write. Because he had experienced several bouts with illness—10 years after his 1910 stroke, he had been stricken with appendicitis and peritonitis (an inflammation of the abdominal cavity)—his doctors had commanded him to slow down. Obediently, he had signed on a partner—a white woman named Helen Moore—to help run his court-reporting business. Moore proved so efficient that Chesnutt had begun leaving most of the work to her, spending more and more time crusading for the causes he believed in, traveling, and vacationing at the family's summer camp in Michigan.

Idlewild, Michigan, some 350 miles north of Cleveland, had become a popular resort area among upper-class blacks. In 1924, Chesnutt built a summer home in this idyllic land of deep lakes, sandy beaches, and towering pines. Here, he indulged in fly-fishing, one of the great passions of his later years; here, he wrote letters and checks in support of such goals as federal antilynching legislation and scholarships for gifted black students. And here, he contemplated the new novel that White had urged him to write.

In 1928, Chesnutt celebrated both his 70th birthday and the 50th year of his marriage to Susan Perry. Writing to thank a friend for sending anniversary flowers, Chesnutt paid a touching tribute to his wife of half a century: "I can imagine marriages where fifty years would seem like an eternity," he said, "but except when I look at my children and see my gray hairs in the mirror, it doesn't seem any time at all, and Mrs. Chesnutt admits that she hasn't found it very tiresome; and we are both willing to hang on a while longer yet."

On June 8, just two days after the golden wedding anniversary, Chesnutt received a thrilling wire. Signed by NAACP chief James Weldon Johnson, it informed the author that he had been named that year's winner of the Spingarn Medal. This put Chesnutt in very good company. Annually awarded for the "highest or noblest achievement by an American Negro," the NAACP's golden trophy had earlier gone

Newton D. Baker, a former Cleveland mayor and U.S. secretary of war, might have become a U.S. Supreme Court justice—if Chesnutt had approved of his nomination in 1932. At that point, NAACP chief Walter White asked Chesnutt about Baker's attitude on the "race question." Baker, responded Chesnutt, was a "fine gentleman," but he had quietly supported several antiblack measures in Cleveland. As a result, the NAACP opposed Baker, and he lost the nomination.

to such great men and women as author and intellectual leader W. E. B. Du Bois, political activist Mary B. Talbert, and botanist George Washington Carver.

Once again, the Chesnutt home was flooded with messages of affection and congratulation. The award "should long ago [have] been given you," asserted Alain Locke. "I know of no one who has accomplished more," said a Cleveland business associate. "You have lived, reared, and educated a fine family [and] added a broader human understanding that will permit future generations to do like wise with more ease and happiness." White writer Carl Van Vechten congratulated not only Chesnutt but the NAACP: "It is my contention," he said in a jubilant telegram, "that the Spingarn Medal Committee has covered itself with glory!"

In early July 1928, Susan and Charles Chesnutt packed their bags and headed for Los Angeles, site of the Spingarn award ceremony. After being com-

Accompanied by friends, Charles and Susan Chesnutt (left) arrive in Los Angeles, California, to accept the NAACP's 1928 Spingarn Medal. The prestigious, long-overdue award delighted Chesnutt's friends and admirers; one, writer Carl Van Vechten, asserted that by giving it to Chesnutt, "the Spingarn Medal Committee . . . covered itself with glory!"

mended for his "distinguished literary service to Afro-Americans," Chesnutt thanked the committee, then launched into a discussion of one of his favorite themes:

> My physical makeup was such that I knew the psychology of people of mixed blood in so far as it differed from that of other people, and most of my writings ran along the color line. . . . It has more dramatic possibilities than life within clearly defined and widely differentiated groups. This was perfectly natural and I have no apologies to make for it.

Returning to Cleveland in triumph, Chesnutt was greeted by more praise, this from the Cleveland *Plain Dealer*:

> [The Spingarn award] is a bestowal fittingly made. Mr. Chesnutt has been an untiring worker for good causes, a writer of strength and grace and sound purpose. Some of his earlier books have been all but forgotten by a generation always eager for the new, but they will long remain as an expression of a brave soul pouring itself out in effective protest against racial prejudice.

Walter White, a much-praised novelist, respected literary critic, celebrated wit, and courageous black rights leader, was also a firm admirer of fellow author Charles Chesnutt. It was at White's suggestion that Chesnutt wrote his final novel, "The Quarry."

Reenergized by this new wave of applause for his fiction, Chesnutt now settled down to write the novel he had promised Walter White. That novel, "The Quarry," focused on Donald Glover, a brilliant and accomplished young man who becomes a leader of New York City's black community. Although Glover, who grows up thinking himself a mulatto, eventually discovers he has no black blood, he believes he can do more good as a black, and elects to conceal the truth and continue to live as "a Negro."

Glover embodied almost every virtue Chesnutt could think of. He was, says William Andrews, "a brilliant student, a marvelous singer, a consummate organist, a charming and irresistible stage presence, a man of taste, culture, sensitivity, modesty, achievement, and purpose." The result: a character who is "a devastating bore, if not an insufferable prig." Trying to keep up with the times, Chesnutt even threw in a few modestly sexy scenes, but these are so "infinitely delicate," observes Andrews, that they are "embarrassing."

Chesnutt's finances had been seriously dented by the 1929 stock market crash. Submitting "The Quarry" to Houghton Mifflin in 1930, he said he hoped for publication not only "for my soul's satisfaction, but because I need the money." He had not, he added, "dredged the sewers of the Negro underworld" to find his characters, but had "rather essayed to depict a cross section . . . of the colored people along the edge of the color line."

Out of step with the times, confusing, and featuring an unbelievably saintlike hero, "The Quarry" was, in short, unpublishable. Politely but firmly, both Houghton Mifflin and the publisher Alfred Knopf rejected it. After this, Chesnutt produced one more piece of fiction: "Concerning Father," an amusing short story published in *The Crisis* magazine in 1930. In this tale, a stuffy, very proper white Boston man goes into a trance and discovers that his great-great-grandmother was a dark-skinned Indian. The story's slender plot hangs on the reaction of the man's family to this "shocking" news from the past.

Chesnutt believed that eventually, most Americans would, as he did, have both black and white blood. Over and over, he created racially mixed characters, using mulattoes as the symbol of the nation's racial future. Perhaps fittingly, the publication of "Concerning Father," a story that centered on interracial bloodlines, marked the end of his literary career.

During the next two years, the author-activist wrote and spoke about public issues, spent an occasional day in his Cleveland office, and relaxed with his family at Idlewild. After 54 years together, he and Susan enjoyed each other's company as much as ever. "A more loyal and devoted wife no man ever had,"

Angler Chesnutt proudly displays a prize catch at his summer home in Idlewild, Michigan. A fishing addict, the author found immense pleasure in the deep, clear lake at the Idlewild resort, where he built a waterfront cottage for himself and his family. His other summer-time pleasures included swimming, boating, and late-night dancing at the resort's clubhouse.

he told a friend. "I've got my job cut out for the rest of my life to make her feel how much I appreciate her devotion."

These days, Chesnutt's step may have been somewhat slower and his hearing a bit weaker, but his spirits and his passionate interest in the world—in family, friends, race relations, literature, politics, and economics—remained undimmed. But one day in mid-November 1932, after visiting the office to con-

With her cat for company, Susan Chesnutt waits for her husband to return from a day of fishing at Idlewild. Even after 50 years of marriage, the Chesnutts' pleasure in each other's company remained bright; as Charles remarked on their golden wedding anniversary, half a century might seem like "an eternity" to some people, but to them, "it [didn't] seem any time at all."

fer with Helen Moore, he felt unusually tired. That night, he told his wife he was going to bed early.

Summoned by a worried Susan Chesnutt, the family doctor came to examine the patient. Noting that Chesnutt's blood pressure was even higher than usual, the doctor called in a nurse to keep an eye on him. Four days later, in the late afternoon of November 15, 1932, the nurse emerged from Chesnutt's room and silently beckoned to Susan Chesnutt and her daughters. He smiled at each of them, then reached out for his wife's hand. Moments later, with a wistful smile on his face, Charles Chesnutt died. He was 72 years old.

The funeral was held in the Chesnutt home. Arriving to pay their last sorrowing respects were friends, relatives, employees, judges, lawyers, and members of the many organizations in which Chesnutt had been an active member. Befitting a service for a man whose life had been dedicated to the cause of equality, the mourners included a cross section of America: the rich and the poor, blacks, whites, Christians, Jews, Protestants, Catholics.

Chesnutt's friends had lost a beloved colleague and tireless champion, but he had gained all he had ever hoped for; he had built his "castle in the air." Chesnutt had found what he once described as his life's goals: "A dear companion to share my joys, a happy family growing up around me, and when having had enough of the world, I pass away to a better, 'my children shall rise up and call me blessed' and I be regretted and remembered with love and respect by all who knew me."

Chesnutt's accomplishments, however, reached far beyond his personal life. Overcoming terrific odds, he refined his magnificent literary gift and became the nation's first black published novelist. In so doing, he shed light on the black experience and dramatized the strength of character blacks showed in enduring racial injustice.

Had he chosen to, the blue-eyed, fair-skinned author could have "passed" and enjoyed the rights whites reserved for themselves. He chose not to. Deeply proud of his own mixed-blood ancestry, Charles Chesnutt demanded that the constitutional guarantee of "life, liberty, and the pursuit of happiness" be extended to all Americans. ✦

APPENDIX: THE BOOKS AND SHORT FICTION OF CHARLES CHESNUTT

The years in which Charles Chesnutt's books and short fiction were first published are listed below. (No record exists of the year when the story "An Original Sentiment" was first published.) The stories "The Conjurer's Revenge," "The Goophered Grapevine," and "Po' Sandy" were subsequently reprinted in The Conjure Woman; *"The Bouquet," "The Sheriff's Children," and "The Wife of His Youth" in* The Wife of His Youth and Other Stories of the Color Line.

1885   "Uncle Peter's House"

1886   "A Bad Night," "The Fall of Adam," "A Secret Ally," "A Tight Boot," "Tom's Warm Welcome"

1887   "Appreciation," "Aunt Lucy's Search," "A Busy Day in a Lawyer's Office," "The Doctor's Wife," "The Goophered Grapevine," "A Grass Widow," "How Dasdy Came Through," "McDugald's Mule," "A Metropolitan Experience," "A Midnight Adventure," "She Reminded Him," "A Soulless Corporation," "A Virginia Chicken," "Wine and Water"

1888   "Cartwright's Mistake," "A Doubtful Success," "An Eloquent Appeal," "A Fool's Paradise," "Gratitude," "How a Good Man Went Wrong," "Po' Sandy"

1889   "The Conjurer's Revenge," "Dave's Neckliss," "A Fatal Restriction," "The Origin of the Hatchet Story," "A Roman Antique," "The Sheriff's Children"

1891   "A Cause Célèbre"

1893   "A Deep Sleeper"

1898   "The Wife of His Youth"

1899   "The Bouquet," *The Conjure Woman* ("The Conjurer's Revenge," "The Goophered Grapevine," "The Gray Wolf's Ha'nt," "Hot-Foot Hannibal," "Mars Jeems's Nightmare," "Po' Sandy," and "Sis Becky's Pickaninny"), *Frederick Douglass, The Wife of His Youth and Other Stories of the Color Line* ("The Bouquet," "Cicely's Dream," "Her Virginia Mammy," "A Matter of Principle," "The Passing of Grandison," "The Sheriff's Children," "Uncle Wellington's Wives," "The Web of Circumstance," and "The Wife of His Youth")

1900   "Aunt Mimy's Son," "The Bunch of Yellow Roses," *The House Behind the Cedars*, "Lonesome Ben," "The Sway-Backed House," "Tobe's Tribulations," "A Victim of Heredity; or, Why the Darkey Loves Chicken"

1901   "The March of Progress," *The Marrow of Tradition*, "The Partners"

1904   "Baxter's Procrustes"

1905   *The Colonel's Dream*

1906   "The Prophet Peter"

1912   "The Doll"

1915   "Mr. Taylor's Funeral"

1924   "The Marked Tree"

1930   "Concerning Father"

CHRONOLOGY

1858   Born Charles Waddell Chesnutt on June 20 in Cleveland, Ohio

1866   Moves to Fayetteville, North Carolina

1872   Becomes student teacher at Howard School in Fayetteville

1877   Appointed teacher at Normal School in Fayetteville

1878   Marries Susan Perry

1879   First daughter, Ethel, is born

1880   Chesnutt is appointed principal of Fayetteville's Normal School; second daughter, Helen, is born

1883   Chesnutt moves to New York City; becomes reporter for Dow, Jones & Company; writes Wall Street gossip column; only son, Edwin, is born; Chesnutt moves to Cleveland; works for Nickel Plate Railroad Company; begins studying law

1885   "Uncle Peter's House" is published

1887   Chesnutt passes Ohio bar examination; sets up office as court stenographer

1889   "What Is a White Man?" is published

1890   Third daughter, Dorothy, is born

1899   *The Conjure Woman, The Wife of His Youth and Other Stories of the Color Line*, and *Frederick Douglass* are published

1900   *The House Behind the Cedars* is published

1901   *The Marrow of Tradition* is published

1903   *The Negro Problem*, containing Chesnutt's essay, "The Disfranchisement of the Negro," is published

1905   *The Colonel's Dream* is published; Chesnutt joins the Committee of Twelve for the Advancement of the Interests of the Negro Race

1909   Attends preliminary meeting of the NAACP

1910   Suffers a stroke

1920   Suffers appendicitis and peritonitis

1928   Receives NAACP's Spingarn Medal

1932   Dies on November 15 at his Cleveland home

FURTHER READING

Andrews, William L. *The Literary Career of Charles W. Chesnutt*. Baton Rouge: Louisiana State University Press, 1980.

Chesnutt, Charles W. *The Colonel's Dream*. New York: Irvington Press, 1977.

———. *The Conjure Woman*. Ann Arbor: University of Michigan Press, 1969.

———. *Frederick Douglass*. New York: Johnson Reprints, 1970.

———. *The House Behind the Cedars*. New York: Macmillan, 1969.

———. *The Marrow of Tradition*. Ann Arbor: University of Michigan Press, 1969.

———. *The Short Fiction of Charles Chesnutt*. Edited and with an introduction by Sylvia Lyons Render. Washington, DC: Howard University Press, 1974.

———. *The Wife of His Youth and Other Stories of the Color Line*. Ann Arbor: University of Michigan Press, 1968.

Chesnutt, Helen Maria. *Charles W. Chesnutt, Pioneer of the Color Line*. Chapel Hill: University of North Carolina Press, 1952.

Ellison, Curtis W., and E. W. Metcalf, Jr. *Charles W. Chesnutt: A Reference Guide*. Boston: Hall, 1980.

Heermance, J. Noel. *Charles W. Chesnutt: America's First Great Black Novelist*. Hamden, CT: Shoe String Press, 1974.

Keller, Frances Richardson. *An American Crusade: The Life of Charles Waddell Chesnutt*. Provo: Brigham Young University Press, 1978.

INDEX

PICTURE CREDITS

The Bettmann Archive: pp. 20, 29, 46, 97; Courtesy of the Bostonian Society/Old State House: p. 60; Cleveland Public Library: pp. 2–3, 3, 10, 16, 24, 27, 30, 35, 42, 48, 52, 69, 77, 92–93, 96, 98, 102, 104; Culver Pictures: pp. 40, 41, 44, 47, 63, 89; Illustration by Clyde O. Deland from "The Wife of His Youth": p. 55; Fisk University: pp. 18, 19, 64; Museum of the City of New York: pp. 13, 37; The New York Historical Society, Bella C. Landauer Collection: p. 72; North Carolina Department of Cultural Resources: pp. 21, 22, 71, 74–75, 84, 101; Schomburg Center for Research in Black Culture, The New York Public Library, Astor, Lenox and Tilden Foundation: pp. 62, 78, 80, 82, 99; Smith College Archives: pp. 66, 76 (top & bottom); UPI/Bettmann: pp. 58, 94; The Western Reserve Historical Society, Cleveland, Ohio: pp. 15, 32, 38, 70, 85, 86.

CLIFF THOMPSON is a New York City–based writer whose work has appeared most recently in *Breaking Ice: An Anthology of Contemporary African-American Fiction*. He holds a degree in English and creative writing from Oberlin College.

NATHAN IRVIN HUGGINS, one of America's leading scholars in the field of black studies, helped select the titles for the BLACK AMERICANS OF ACHIEVEMENT series, for which he also served as senior consulting editor. He was the W.E.B. Du Bois Professor of History and of Afro-American Studies at Harvard University and the director of the W.E.B. Du Bois Institute for Afro-American Research at Harvard. He received his doctorate from Harvard in 1962 and returned there as a professor in 1980 after teaching at Columbia University, the University of Massachusetts, Lake Forest College, and the California State University, Long Beach. He was the author of four books and dozens of articles, including *Black Odyssey: The Afro-American Ordeal in Slavery*, *The Harlem Renaissance*, and *Slave and Citizen: The Life of Frederick Douglass*, and was associated with the Children's Television Workshop, National Public Radio, the Boston Athenaeum, the Museum of Afro-American History, the Howard Thurman Educational Trust, and Upward Bound. Professor Huggins died in 1989, at the age of 62, in Cambridge, Massachusetts.